EARTHQUAKE KITTEN KISS

Michael Warren Lucas

Tilted
Windmill
Press

My gratitude to Michael Bellomo, Felicia Fredlund, David H. Hendrickson, Michael Kowal, Juliet Nordeen, Mary Raichle, Kris Rusch, Ben Sawyer, and Kelly Shire.

For EAL.

1

I seriously enjoy contracts with Nguyen Chen. His scheduling is meticulous, leaving plenty of time to get used to the time zone in whatever forsaken hellhole we'll be ripping through. Like Burma, or the Congo, or Pittsburgh. Yes, I can do a twelve-hour time shift and hit the ground running fast enough to dodge incoming fire, but that's only because I've got bad-ass physical and mental reserves. I'd rather reserve that energy for actual work.

Chen trusts me. Well, as much as he trusts anyone. His very name is a lie, but a seemingly full-blood American Indian who offers a name like Nguyen is announcing *I'm not going to insult you by telling you a lie you might accidentally believe.* Almost nobody in the trade is crazy enough to use their real name, like I do.

He sent me an encrypted mission briefing before I got on the plane for Ecuador, so I could spend my time reading and studying the objective, terrain, and opposition rather than sneering at the peasants back in steerage or choking my nosy seatmate unconscious when nobody's looking.

Well, maybe thirty seconds of sneering. I'm human.

Chen's never made a pass at me. Not sure if that's because he respects me, if he looks at me and says *oh hell no*, or if he's afraid of letting me close enough to grab him. But that's just another kind of respect.

Some contract organizers and new teammates ask a whole bunch of stupid questions. Can you really put a bullet through someone's head at two miles? Did you really drive out of the Pentagon with half of the Black Library? The *good* half? And got a colonel to open the gate for you? That story about you smacking down one hundred sixteen Marines in a row, did you really—

Yes, *really*. I am *the* Liza Bradley, and you can fuck off.

Okay, my teammates kind of exaggerated the Marines story. It was only forty-six, and I broke my pinky doing it. We were in a corridor, so I only had to open one jarhead at a time. Not as impressive as it sounds.

Hey, the Marines had their chance at me. The maximum weight for a female five foot two Marine is one hundred thirty-seven pounds. I couldn't get down to that if they surgically removed thirty pounds of muscles and both my femurs.

Their loss.

I should be used to dumb questions. Back in middle school I already needed a custom-made bra, because regular stores didn't carry ones that could go around my ribs. For fat girls, sure. But not bras for my Neanderthal hormonal corkscrew.

One of the star football players asked me if I was King of the Dwarves.

That jackass never walked right again.

But nobody in the whole school system ever said a word about my build again. Or my face.

To my face, at least.

Or asked me to the prom—but I shouldn't have even hoped for that. It's not that I'm ugly. I'm built square, unbreakable. Like a brick house.

Go ahead. Play that song. I dare you.

Chen's questions have a whole different theme. Plan clarifications? Equipment adequate? Other concerns? He assumes I know what I'm doing. If I bring up a problem, he listens. He adapts. If it's a real problem, the plan changes.

Truly a joy to work with.

Plus, he hires the best people he can get. Price is always an object, but real pros know what they're worth, and our rates travel faster than gossip. You don't get the call unless they're willing to pay.

But sometimes, the best people you can get aren't very good.

And this new kid is gonna get us all killed.

2

This sprawling Ecuadoran safe house seems tailor-built for us. It's on a peak above Multitud, a so-called town that's basically a couple shops along the road that twists and convulses through the Andes. We've got lots of private rooms. Incredible visibility across the equatorial peaks, surrounded by greenery so thick and tight you couldn't get through with a chainsaw and an oil tanker of Agent Orange. Even if one of the team wanted to go down to the bug-infested shack the locals call a *taberna* for a bottle of Toxic Liver Killer, the only way down is by rappelling or helicopter.

I don't know if Chen's rented the place, stolen it, blackmailed it, or flat-out owns it. I don't really care.

I love that the back porch has a whole bunch of tatami mats.

Our mission, our intrusion, doesn't start for thirty-four and a half hours.

And everybody's bored stiff.

Tarmack and I are swapping joint locks—not at nearly full strength or speed, just stretching our joints and keeping in practice. It's a simple game. The winner grabs the last loser. The person grabbed goes for a lock—say, capturing the thumb, or an outside wrist turn, or something fancy like a little hip throw. The other person escapes, and counters with their own lock.

If you repeat a lock you've already done? You lose.

Can't get out of a lock? You lose.

Lose control and injure your opponent? You lose, and Chen has me kick your ass.

Tarmack's got a couple inches on me, but he's not nearly so muscled—he's a runner, not a cinderblock like me. He doesn't have nearly the strength to *force* me into most of these locks, but that's not the point. In a real fight, he'd break my pelvis with a kick or I'd shatter his skull with the palm of my hand.

This is about skill. Control. Relaxation. Sensitivity.

It's Tai Chi for bone-breakers.

Right now, I've locked Tarmack up twice. He's gotten me twice.

It's the bone-breaker tie-breaker.

We've each gone through eighty-six different finger, wrist, elbow, knee, and shoulder locks in about three minutes, transforming one hold to another like we'd rehearsed this sequence for years even though we're synthesizing it together. Even at the top of a mountain, with cooling breezes from the distant Pacific, the tropical heat leaves us both sweating and slippery and gasping. The rough tatami beneath our feet feels slick with our pooled sweat.

Two people, sharing their bodies with each other to practice mastery of the human form. It's glorious.

The greatest, most incredible intimacy I've ever known.

I almost never get to practice with someone that can push me this hard, and the struggle to remember a technique I haven't yet used this round fills me with fierce joy. I'm tired—not exhausted, I wouldn't short a client that way, but my short hair is a sodden mess and the sweat makes everything more difficult.

It's years of skill coming together in a unique, never-to-be-repeated performance.

But in the background, outside our majestic little ballet of controlled almost-violence, there's a voice. I've never heard this voice before. Don't know who it is. But Chen said "the data kid," one Matt Harrison, was on his way. Ex-Marine, but green as lettuce and half as tough.

"A knee pick? I know that."

"I could break that, just straighten my arm and I'd be out."

"That'd never work, not in the *real* world."

But when he declares, "Wait, she didn't do anything, what was that?" I have officially *had* it.

The kid couldn't even see it, but Tarmack knew damn well that another ounce of pressure and he'd spend the next month wiping his ass with his off hand.

It's as if we're having a beautiful meal in an unexpectedly fantastic restaurant, and someone at the next table has dead skunk farts and sewer breath.

I relax my elbow a vital degree, letting Tarmack slip into the obvious, elementary shoulder crank. His bushy eyebrows arch in surprise, but he lets me have the setup. Like I've planned a really spectacular counter, and he can't wait see what it is.

I hate disappointing him, but slap my chest with my free hand. "Tap, Tarmack."

Tarmack releases me instantly, mouth slack in puzzlement.

"Three rounds to two." I bow. "You win."

Tarmack's shocked now. His face is fascinatingly ugly, like his mom whacked him with a rusty shovel blade every morning before giving him titty. But he steps back and bows in return, a perfect gentleman on the mats.

One afternoon last year we did three thousand falls, celebrating the conclusion of a notably profitable contract. That afternoon he went from joy to stubbornness to determination to mule-headed endurance to, finally, accepting that he couldn't stand again.

To be fair, two more falls and I wouldn't have gotten up again either. One of us had to keep enough strength to fetch the water.

I respect the hell out of Tarmack, and he me.

"Huh," the peanut gallery says. "I coulda got out of that."

I know that Shelley, one of our teammates, has watched the whole thing in silent appreciation. I also know that he's ignored the kid's whole commentary.

I take a deep breath, like I'm tired. "Hey kid!" I say.

Tarmack's misshapen eyebrows shoot up with comprehension, and not a little glee.

"You talking to me?" he says.

"You think you got this?" I turn to look. "How about you play the loser?"

3

I see the newbie, Matt Harrison, and I feel a little quiver.

The damned kid is gorgeous.

About five foot ten or so, maybe eight inches on me, twenty-four years old, with the musculature of a cross-training athlete who stretches as much as he lifts and runs. Eyes this startling blue. Straight, gleaming white teeth. Hair cut short, except on top, where he's left it a little longer and put some sort of crap in to make it stand on end.

Back in high school, he probably got any girl he wanted.

If I saw him in a Hollywood flick, I'd swear he was computer-generated.

He's even got—wait for it—a goddamn *dimple.* Right on his square chin.

And this is his first freelance mission. Ever.

Chen said the stupid kid did four years in the Marines—but as a data tech. He ran computers.

I like ex-Marine teammates. Give me a guy who's seen buddies die of IEDs or sniper fire or unexpected shelling, he knows the important things.

People are fragile.

Our services: Theft. Betrayal. Destruction. Death.

Even in tomorrow night's seemingly straightforward in-and-out, there's a good chance someone won't wake up the next day.

Afterwards, you walk away from the dying. You go home and practice harder, so you don't become another corpse.

But apparently a Marine that spent four years studying network security systems is as dumb as a crate of kittens.

Harrison doesn't even know enough to keep his mouth shut.

Chen said that Harrison's a year younger than me physically, but he clearly has no clue how fragile we all are.

He's leaning against one of the screened-in porch's support pillars, in prime position for the mountain breeze to cool his back. Somehow he makes the khaki shorts and dark brown tight T-shirt look hand-selected by a highly paid Parisian fashionista.

He meets my eyes without blinking or looking away, I'll give him that. Most people can't help looking at me and reacting somehow, even if it's just a blink of surprise.

Harrison's voice is deep, too. If he quit freelancing, he could get a gig doing voice-overs for action movies. "I don't do all those fancy locks, ma'am. They taught me practical stuff."

Six weeks of basic training isn't even enough time to teach you to keep your hands up. I wipe my damp palms on my terrycloth shorts. The shorts are pretty wet, so it doesn't help much. "All right then. How about take-downs? Any grab, any take-down, early tap? Pull-punch sparring?"

"He is merely the data guy," Tarmack says. "We're supposed to keep him from fighting."

Harrison raises his chin. What a macho little kitten. "I can fight, sir."

"Fight?" I say. "This is a slap fight. A few falls. Show me your moves."

Doubt, or maybe wisdom, flickers in those deep eyes. "My contract says no combat."

"Who's in combat?" I say. "It's a pre-mission workout."

"Leave Mister Harrison be," Tarmack says. "He is not your skill level."

It's not quite the oldest trick in the book, but I'm pretty sure Caveman Og pulled the same shtick back in the day. What makes it a better shtick, of course, is that Tarmack is speaking the complete truth.

Harrison straightens. "Just a few falls."

I step back and hold out a hand to the far side of the mat.

I don't want to hurt him.

Really, I'm helping him.

If he learns to shut up, if he can study his betters, he might learn something.

He might even survive this mission, or this career.

But as he unties his shoes and peels his socks away, there's this mocking hilarity bubbling in my soul.

Lessons like this can be a lot of fun. For the teacher.

A pretty boy like that normally wouldn't look at me.

And I can't help enjoying that this pretty boy is gonna learn to watch out for women like me.

Harrison's first steps on the mats are tentative. Christ, even his feet are perfect: straight sliced nails with only a sliver of white, no callouses I can see, not even any scale of athlete's foot. Does he get pedicures or something?

I suddenly feel embarrassed of my own feet. I take a men's size twelve shoe, wide, because they're a lot easier to find than a women's fifteen. My toenails are a little ragged. My right foot has a dry, flaking patch between my big toe and the next. And my callouses are like turtle shell.

Screw embarrassment. This kitten needs someone to pick him up by the scruff of the neck.

I draw my heels together. Place my right fist in the open palm of my left. Keep my focus on Harrison, and execute a perfect bow.

Harrison keeps his feet shoulder width apart, claps his hands together like he's at church or something, and gives this sketchy half-bow, his eyes not meeting mine. His nervousness is delicious.

I stand straight and raise my hands, palms open, facing him.

Harrison raises his paws. Fists. Whatever.

We stand a few yards apart, studying each other.

I offer a little nod. "Whenever you're ready."

Harrison doesn't need much goading, but comes at me with a giant haymaker. It's a feint, of course, meant to distract me from the other hand lashing out to catch my shirt.

But I'm already not there, I've pivoted out of the way. My hand finds his shoulder and yanks while my shin sweeps out against his calf.

Harrison's back hits the ground before he can blink, his arms and legs trailing wildly. He looks even more like a kitten, an offended one, as his jaw clanks shut with the impact.

I bring my knee up and swivel my hip in a viciously fast stomp kick.

Harrison's eyes get huge as my heel flashes at his face.

I pull it maybe an inch short and pivot back. "Keep your mouth closed, kitten. How can you smooth-talk the ladies if you bite your tongue off in a fall?"

The stunned look in his eyes gets incinerated in a flash of fury.

Some Marines shouldn't believe their own press.

Harrison would be a pleasure to practice with, if he had any idea what he was doing. He's got all that lovely muscle and incredible flexibility.

Giving him one hard fall is enough. For the next five minutes, I let him get up. I let him grab me, seize me, rush me, take a swing at me.

And I put him down.

Gently.

Just like a kitten.

He's tough, I'll give him that. Most people do one fall and they can't get up. A few can do five, or a dozen.

At fifteen, he gets tired enough to slow down. I see him try to think before each grab or strike. Good.

I'm careful not to hurt him. One, there's a job tomorrow—but two, bruising him up would be like spray-painting a Michelangelo. Just because he won't look at me doesn't mean I can't look at him.

My initial amusement's past. I'm playing—he's serious, but to me he's serious like a six-year-old black belt. He needs to understand all the way down to his bones that he doesn't know jack, he can't fight his way out of a paper bag, but the joy of dominating him has faded into my joy of my craft.

Firearms are great tools. But for sheer thrills, there's nothing like another person's hands grabbing on to you and refusing to let go.

At thirty falls, the kitten's gasping. But he doesn't quit.

Somehow, by thirty-five, he's got his breath back under control.

I'm unwillingly impressed.

I don't throw him hard. If I break a sweat, it means I have to work to put him down. The lesson he needs demands that I make it look easy.

For me, it's a cool-down. I even start to pick up the nasty vinegar stink of drying sweat.

His bright eyes narrow when he picks up that reek. I can see his thoughts on his face. Maybe my little smile's okay, but if I'm cooling down *that* much when he throws himself at me, well, that's just rude.

But he won't give up.

If the kitten grows up a little, if he learns to control himself, he just might be good at this. He's got the body, and that tenacity's pretty amazing.

Somehow, he makes it to eighty-one falls.

He gets back up eighty-one times.

I have my hands up in front of my face. Not in surrender, but to protect myself from a blow.

This is the kitten's eighty-second chance to bow out.

He grabs my wrists and goes for a throw.

I swivel my hands and pivot around to throw him over my back—

—and the whole world moves.

Sadly, that's not a metaphor.

4

A grumbling, rumbling sound fills the porch, a basso growl that makes the breeze itself seem to shudder to a halt.

The tatami mats dissolve beneath me.

I shift a foot, struggling to hold my balance, but Harrison's grip on my wrists has suddenly gotten a whole bunch tighter, his weight on my back no longer in my control, or his, or anyone's. And there's nothing solid to stand on.

Tarmack swears in Spanish. I'd completely forgotten he was there. My Spanish isn't that great, but I remember the word *terremoto*.

Earthquake.

This place is perched on top of a mountain.

I don't scare easy, but bright fear blooms in my gut. I can fight anyone— but I can't fight the Earth, I can't stand against a mountain top that decides to go spend a few million years in the valley.

Plus, I have the world's heaviest kitten on my back.

The tatami mats slide on the vibrating floor, the shaking world, and I tumble down.

Somehow, I wrench around to turn my plunge into a back fall.

If I die here, it'll be face up.

Harrison crashes down on top of me.

My whole art is based on touch, on sensitivity. Even a sniper rifle demands touch. The shaking earth scrambles my senses and leaves me wildly disoriented, confused like a mouse in free fall, unable to understand even how to move.

Harrison doesn't knock the breath out of me—a full grown bull moose dropped from orbit couldn't do that.

But I can't get up, there's no traction.

Harrison's nose is jammed into my ear. His free hand clutches my shoulder—not technique, no technique at all, only desperate senseless mewling. His long, muscular form sprawls on top of me, his hip plunged between my thighs.

The world moving around us, the whole house ready to plunge down a mountain—I'm helpless, like I haven't been since I was a babe in my dad's arms.

Trapped in shifting unreality

The only solid thing here: Harrison.

I'm desperate for something to hold on to, some solid thing that I can use to orient myself. My jackrabbit heart demands to flee.

I'm adrift.

I pull guard.

That's when you wrap your legs around your opponent's body, locking your ankles together to pin them in place.

His arms engulf my back.

We're adrift in space, blasted into the ever-shifting Twilight Zone with nothing but each other.

For the first time in my adult life, I'm in a man's arms and neither of us is trying to throw, maim, or kill the other. The whole world quakes around us. Shattered plaster rains from the ceiling and dust fills the air. And my clumsy clench with Harrison is the only solid thing in the universe.

Out in the churning void, something explodes. Dynamite? Grenade?

No. Bigger than that.

If the earthquake doesn't take the mountain down, we've got enough munitions up here to do the job ourselves.

The memory of our explosives expert checking the incendiary kits flashes through my brain. Please, let Klaver not have prepped anything already, *please*.

I don't even know who I'm begging.

Harrison wrenches his nose out of my ear to clutch me closer. His cheek is soft on mine. Warm. He's shaved, so recently that there's not even any stubble, the kind of shave you only get with an old-fashioned bladed razor and hot soap. His hair is full of sweat, absolutely drenched, but somehow has this weird spicy-sweet smell that triggers primal wiring buried in my brainstem.

Suddenly, my heart's hammering with a whole new kind of terror.

5

The shifting cosmos vibrates and shudders.

Through the roar of the world remaking itself I hear a horrific clatter of falling wood—I'd call it a crash, except now there's the clang of metal striking metal, but there's no big chunks of metal around unless it's the frame of the building itself, and I'm totally completely helplessly terrified.

That's nothing compared to the horrible, *appalling* shift inside me.

I want Harrison closer. He's the only real thing in the world and I want to wrap myself around him, dive into him, clutch every contour of muscle and that meticulously groomed skin and pull him into me.

My arms clamp around Harrison's back. I can't possibly yank him closer, but he isn't going anywhere, not until there's something else solid in the universe. He's shifted to squeeze his hard abs, those incredible pecs, right up against me.

Nothing in the world is solid but us.

But through the terror, this little voice inside me is cursing his shirt, my shirt, every scrap of clothing I own. My hands knot themselves into the frustrating, infuriating T-shirt—

The shirt's not part of us. It rips apart like paper.

My hands clamp onto his back.

He's sweaty and hard in my hands, and as my fingers dig in that long-buried voice shrieks atavistic demands from my brainstem, from my heart, from places further down.

I'm suddenly aware of that unexplored universe inside me. One I've tried to ignore. One I've known damn well I will never be able to explore. I've mastered my body in so many ways—but that unexplored void screams at me now, demanding I plunge into it as I clutch at Harrison and his incredible, protective arms surround me.

I've been fighting since kindergarten! I do *not* need protection.

The titanic growl climbs. The outside world shakes, but that's nothing next to the planets colliding in my soul. Harrison is just so—damned—*alive* in my arms, between my legs.

The vibration stops like someone flipped a switch.

The basso roar rolls away, echoing through mountain valleys.

Harrison's still clamped around me. Not a grappling clench, but he's got his own aftershocks. And my ankles are still locked around him, my heels digging into that fine ass.

Fine ass? What the *fuck*?

But I can't make myself release him.

We're both gasping. My hands are clamped onto his bare shoulder blades, my fingernails dug into his skin, somehow clenching the muscles. I'm queasy, but not from the earth's motion.

I force out a shuddering breath and jerk my right hand away from his smooth, sweat-slicked skin. Straightening those fingers takes a deliberate, focused effort of will. I ache to hold him, clutch him close, but—no.

That is not my universe.

And if I ever do decide to explore that, it wouldn't be with a mewling kitten.

Harrison draws a shuddering breath himself. If I'm shook up, he must be downright scrambled.

His broad chest shifting against mine sends an unfamiliar, delicious shiver down my spine.

I shove the shiver away. *That is not your life.*

Harrison unlocks his own muscles one at a time. His hands, sliding off my back, leave little trails of desolation. But in another shaky breath—his? mine?—he's raised himself onto his hands.

My legs still clasp him, ankles loosely interlocked. I just haven't gotten around to letting him go yet. Really.

Harrison draws a breath, looking down at me. He's struggling for something to say, something to brush all this away, something to refocus himself back on the world. It's part of getting yourself together. A drop of sweat slides down his face and hangs heavy from one side of his chin, right next to that damn dimple.

"So," he wheezes. A ramshackle smirk props up one side of his full lips. "Was it good for you?"

That dangling drop of sweat slips free, hitting my cheek right below my eye. It runs down my face like a tear.

It's like he's seen straight into my soul. Peered right into a secret place that I'd hidden, even from myself, for my entire whole life.

A place I denied. Because even if I wanted it, nobody would ever want to go there with me.

His words are a catalyst, instantly transforming my confusion over that sudden, unwanted discovery into something much more familiar, incredibly more comfortable.

All-consuming rage.

How dare he? How *dare* he?

My ankles tighten into each other like clamps, cranking Harrison's spine right down onto me. I knock his supporting hand away, and he comes plummeting back down, but before he hits I bump my hips up and he's plunging forward, unbalanced. I bump again and roll us both over. A quick elbow to the inside of his thigh, a twist of an arm, and I'm straddling his chest.

During practice, I usually take a fraction of my weight on my knees.

Not this time.

My heart pounds in my throat, in my temples.

Harrison's eyes are wide, surprised. At least his mouth is closed, his teeth together. But he hasn't brought his elbows down to his side, so I shoot forward, wedging my knees into his armpits and settling my bulk right on the edge of his ribcage, right along the pressure point where his diaphragm seizes up.

His mouth opens now. His last air wheezes out like a stabbed tire.

"Listen to me, kitten," I growl. "You are soft. If you don't learn to shut up, you will die. Maybe they'll kill you." I lean forward, bringing my face as close to his as I can without surrendering position. "But if your blabbering, if your *ego*, gets another team member so much as a scratch…"

I reach down with one finger. I'm planning to run my nail straight across his throat, the simplest word of the universal human language.

Instead, my traitorous fingertip touches the outside corner of his eyelid. Right by one of those incredible, rich blue eyes.

Those eyes look as wide as his flapping, airless mouth.

My rage isn't pure any more. My guts have this horrible tangle of passion, of desires, of needs I've always indulged and needs I've always denied.

Harrison's terrified.

It's perfect.

It's horrible.

He's got to know.

It's not what I want to say.

I don't even know how to *think* what I want to say.

My finger gently traces down his face, along the hollow of his cheek.

Dust is already soaking into his sweat, coating that luscious smooth skin in grit. My touch brushes it aside, just hardly touching him, as I trail the touch down to his chin.

I've always thought that sometimes the worst threats are understated. I'm not sure if my touch is a tender caress, or a promise of violence. Or both.

My finger stops right at that adorable dimple.

Pulling the hand back leaves a tingle at the tip of that finger.

"Anyone gets hurt," I whisper into his face, "and I will kill you myself."

Harrison's ribs twitch beneath me.

Parts of me twitch in response.

"Nod if you understand," I whisper.

His chin spasms up once, twice.

That's enough. He's got his lesson.

That's not enough. Not nearly enough.

The unquenchable heat of his chest burns up through my thighs.

And it's not even close to what I want.

But it's all I'm ever going to have.

I shift my weight to one side. Harrison heaves air like he'd been drowning.

Or like a brick home had been sitting on his chest.

I rise to my feet on the crumpled mat floor. Tatami always has a rough texture, but now my bare feet crunch in dust and chunks of plaster.

Harrison lies on his back for one, two, three breaths. Color's oozing back into his face.

I reach a hand down. "Come on, Kitten. Let's see what's going on."

Harrison tries to get an elbow beneath him. Sweat streaks the dust and plaster powder on his face. And that shirt? Ruined.

"We're teammates." I shake my hand impatiently, keeping my face still: not frowning, not smiling. "We help each other. You know the rules. Let's get to work."

He studies my face for half a breath, then reaches up to clasp my hand.

I do my best to ignore the tingle that runs up my arm at his touch.

Not going to happen. Cannot happen.

Fantasy gets people killed.

6

Night falls early in the valleys, but late on the mountaintops.

To my surprise, our mountaintop was still a mountaintop. We had lots of light to work by, even if the solar panels were gone.

No, not broken—gone. The mountains aren't a fault line, but you can't knock a million billion tons of rock around without some of it breaking off. The solar panels, the rear outbuilding, the abandoned goat pen, all of that's a couple thousand feet below us.

As are the bedrooms.

Fortunately, the only one asleep at the time was Klaver. Not so fortunate for him, sure, but the rest of us lucked out. In a thousand years, maybe someone'll find his bones.

Searching the wreckage for our remaining resources, to identify the damage, keeps me busy. No, not too busy to think—I'm always thinking.

Too busy to *feel*.

Too busy to listen to my traitorous body.

Tarmack's got this brutal bruise on his left forearm, where part of the ceiling fell. It's one thing to be good at a martial art, at throwing and taking a strike. It's another thing entirely to have a roof fall on you, during an earthquake, and perform a *chudan* block with the correct part of your arm.

Mentally, I upgrade Tarmack to "really, truly *serious* bad-ass."

We were damn lucky.

Somehow, the cistern is still a quarter full. We heat enough water for everyone to have a sponge bath. There's a whole world of difference between "alive and healthy" versus "alive, healthy, and not filthy with soot and sweat."

It's not the first sponge bath I've taken. It's certainly not going to be the last.

But somehow, in that little alcove formed by the remains of the imploded staff kitchen, the hot water and soap feels... different. Drops of water trace delicate, tickling trails down my legs, my back, my buttocks.

Fucking Harrison.

No, I snarl at myself. Not Harrison. It was an earthquake, my first one. I know damn well that people have... extreme reactions to impending death. I thought I had a deal with death, that death was something I handed out, that I enjoy the struggle... but really, death shows up for everyone.

And when death peeks at you, the old survive-procreate instinct kicks in.

There's a joy in the fight. A joy in survival.

I survived.

So enjoy getting clean, I tell myself. I'm alive. Klaver's dead. It could have been the other way around.

I seize the sponge, plunge it into the water, and squeeze it against my cheek.

There's a little tingle. Like when Harrison's cheek pressed into mine, right there.

The water dripping off my chin feels like gentle fingers trailing down the slope of my breasts.

I erupt in a string of profanities, plunge the sponge back into the coffee-hot water, and brutally scrub myself like I'm a freshly used roasting pan. The red scratches left in my skin feel tender, but it's the right sort of tender, like I'd rolled down a hill of brambles.

I have several changes of clothes. Instead of the relaxed clothes suitable for a quiet evening, I armor myself in tough camo pants, a tougher khaki shirt, a mesh belt ready to take equipment, and heavy boots.

I come out of the makeshift bath ready for war, thrusting the empty bucket at Tarmack before stomping off.

Too bad this enemy doesn't care about uppercuts or bullets.

7

Chen and Shelley build a fire out on the patio, fueled by the grand hall's couch. It's lightly lacquered mahogany, cut a century ago. Hard wood like that will burn for a year.

More small fires decorate the shattered foothills beneath us. Previous nights had a rich canopy of stars, the few scattered bits of electric light below unable to touch the glorious tropical Milky Way and the sliver of dying moon, but tonight Ecuador's reliving the Spanish conquest. Complete with dysentery and cholera, if help doesn't arrive soon.

The ash- and dust-laden breeze grows cooler. This part of the Andes isn't tall enough to have snow, but the air acquires a definite chill.

We finish dragging equipment out into the slanted yard and settle down for a meal of five-star ready meals. Most organizers would have gone straight to US Army surplus "Meals, Ready to Eat," usually called "three lies in a can," but Chen gets the French stuff every time. I don't even care what flavor it is, just grab one. A little water in the bag, squish it around, pull the heat tab, and when I unscrew the top two minutes later the smell of beef and noodles in garlic and red wine sauce hits my nose.

Ambrosia.

Ambrosia in a foil bag, sure.

But after today it hits my stomach like mother's milk with added wine.

I suck it down, barely bothering to chew, keeping my eyes on the fire flickering between priceless mahogany splinters and spars.

I like watching fire. It's the video track for meditation.

I'm definitely not avoiding looking at Kitten, sitting across the fire. He cleaned up just fine, getting the dust off his face. His new shirt is long-sleeved, but tight, hugging those firm biceps and his pecs.

No, it's that I *love* looking at the fucking fire.

Chen's long face seems almost horsey in the firelight. He no longer resembles a man escaped from a drug-plagued Indian reservation. Perched cross-legged on an inverted plastic bin only feet from the fire, he's another throwback to the conquest. If General Custer had seen the firelight flickering up into Chen's face, he would have had second, third, and fourth thoughts about the whole Little Big Horn thing.

Finishing his meal, Chen sips from a bottle of water before saying "Status?"

"Weapons are all fine," I say. Some organizers would have brought weapons and tools in duffel bags, but Chen had shipped everything wrapped in soft cloth and tucked into custom cut foam inside metal cases. The weapons might have fallen down the mountain, but in that packaging they would have ended up a hell of a lot better than poor Klaver.

Next to me, Tarmack says, "Penetration gear accounted for. Self-tests, they are all *bien*." The man is fantastically ugly. I mean, you could put him up as the poster child for "don't drink or drug while pregnant."

I wonder if he's ever had a girlfriend.

No, an ugly man with gobs of money and that dangerous air, he's all set. He's probably got a pair of trophy wives stashed in a mansion somewhere.

With that three-thousand-falls-in-an-afternoon-for-fun physical stamina, he probably *needs* two. Poor things probably have to tag-team each other and beg him to find a piece on the side for one night a week.

What am I *thinking*?

I want to slap myself.

Phil Broadwell isn't nearly as muscular as Tarmack or I, but he has this easy natural grace and coordination. He's a gunbunny, but doubles as our field medic. (An actual trained field medic? Have I mentioned how much I *adore* working with Chen?) With a grab I could put Broadwell down hard, but he'd put a bullet between my eyes before I got halfway there. It'd be best to take him out from a mile or two. From behind.

"Medically," Broadwell drawls, "y'all came out lucky. Klaver's long gone. Worst injury we've got is Tarmack's arm. I've drained the wound enough to keep it from swelling up." His Texas accent comes and goes. I'm not sure if he pretends to be Texan, or he pretends *not* to be, or if he's just screwing with us.

Either way, I can appreciate that sense of humor.

I shake myself, trying to refocus.

What the steaming fresh hell is *wrong* with me?

No, I know what's wrong.

I have to shove that part of myself back into its box. I *must*.

The world outside me is far larger, and far more brutal, than any world inside me.

And for a woman built like a cross between a linebacker and a gorilla?

Far, far crueler.

Shut it down, girl. Get your act together.

Chen turns to Shelley.

Shelley's black skin gleams in the dark. His hair's cut too short to curl, a shadow against the star-spattered sky. In those dark clothes, he's invisible against the wrecked house behind him. "I can't find one case of detonators, and we're down one box of plastique. Rest of the incendiaries are fine. I'm thinking the rest are with Klaver."

Not one inappropriate thought about Shelley. Better.

I can beat this.

The ring is silent.

Chen says, "Harrison?"

I look over just in time to see Kitten jump at being poked. Was he staring at me? Has he been looking at me the whole time I'm looking in the fire? "Data gear is fine. Everything boots, everything runs, all fully charged. My part of the job's simple, anyway."

"I didn't ask how complicated your task was," Chen says, without hostility. He's good at telling people the rules without intimidating them.

Kitten glances at me then. His mouth opens like he's going to say something, then he clamps those large lips together and looks into the fire.

I think that's fear in his eyes.

Good, I tell myself.

But those averted blue eyes knock holes in my soul.

Leaving empty spaces.

8

"Radio says that the earthquake hit hard in Guayaquil," Chen says, using a busted mahogany table leg to stir fresh cinders and a hint of burned varnish from the fire. "The target area's included."

Guayaquil is Ecuador's biggest port. It's a colorful concrete city, full of lively people, weekend food festivals, and docks constantly shipping bananas and shrimp across the world.

Kitten stares into the fire. He's still afraid, but there's an ill twist to his mouth, like he's eaten something bad and it's kicking his guts from the inside.

I hate that look on him.

"My plan said tomorrow night," Chen continues. "The soldiers around the seized plant, they've almost certainly been pulled up to Guayaquil. Even if Quito did not order it, an isolated on-site commander would almost certainly send most of his men to assist, retaining only a minimal staff."

I have no right to have an opinion on a teammate's appearance. This is not an ogle-the-pretty-toy-soldier moment. My thoughts shred under a barrage of swearing at myself.

"By tomorrow," Chen continues, "the Army will enter Guayaquil in force. The Red Cross will arrive. The soldiers dedicated to the target site will return, and have reinforcements near at hand. I scheduled the operation for tomorrow night, but that will no longer work."

Chen pokes the fire. Cinders swirl, to be carried away on the dusty wind. "Our transportation is intact. I've summoned it. My decision now is: do we proceed immediately, even one man down? Or do we return the client's money and go our separate ways?"

Chen's the boss. It's his decision.

But he's asking for our thoughts.

I've never quit halfway through a contract. I've thought about it, yes. I've walked out during the planning stage, when it became clear that the whole thing was a monster clusterfuck that would get us all killed. I tried to walk off the last one, but my old buddy Rob takes debts really, really seriously.

But once the mission is on, I am all-in.

But right now, my guts scream for me to recommend quitting.

Earthquakes come under any Acts of God clause. Clients aren't always rational, but they accept that when the earth opens up and swallows your chopper and half your team, the mission is a bust.

But we've got the gear. We've got transport. We should go.

And earthquakes have aftershocks. If we stay, the ground might kill us.

But that's all rationalizations.

Kitten's looking even more sick now.

That kid should not be here.

Worse, working with him threatens me. I didn't realize that before, but when Chen suggested the vague possibility of a scrub, everything in me leapt at the chance.

Kitten's forlorn form across the fire pulls at me. It's not that he's scared—I can encourage or insult or cajole scared teammates into action.

I need a second to realize what's happened inside me.

I don't want to see that handsome face hurt.

My breath catches, just a little, and I feel my eyes get wide.

This is utter bullshit.

Is one moment of instinctive reaction going to ruin my career, my life? Fill me with stupid, soft, totally bogus desires? Things that a woman that looks like me cannot ever have? What am I supposed to do, start knitting baby bulletproof vests?

Chill, I tell myself. It was only hours ago, I tell myself. Remember the first time I saw a partner take a bullet? That messed me up for a couple days. The first time I shot someone, I drank vodka for a day. I broke that first neck, and I—hell, I don't even remember what I did then.

I stayed alive. That's what I did. That's what I do.

One cute guy?

All right, fine. He *is* cute. I can admit that. Handsome, even, although that damn dimple pushes him over the top into you-have-to-be-kidding-me.

In a day or two, the raw immediacy, that shocking intimacy? It'll pass.

Maybe some more vodka.

No, we're in Ecuador. Tequila? What do they drink here, anyway?

The next time I'm throwing a handsome, athletic, dimpled man with shockingly clear blue eyes and enough willpower to get up eighty-one times in a row, and an earthquake hits right then, I'll be ready.

Hell, I'll laugh off the earthquake and finish the throw.

But I didn't quit that first mission just because I shot a man in the chest, and missed his heart, and he kicked and made that horrible sound before he died, did I? No, I went and made sure I learned the proper mercy for my career.

A clean shot, right through the ticker.

What's the proper mercy for this?

Maybe I'll hire a cute guy. A professional, one who knows what he's doing. Find out what all the fuss is about.

If it's dark, I won't have to see his face when he looks at me.

Suddenly I realize that everyone's looking at me. I couldn't have been thinking more than a second or two, but Chen's head is cocked and his eyes are curious. Tarmack is frowning. Shelley seems amused. Broadwell seems prepared to wait forever for the lady to speak.

Everyone else has already offered their advice, and I didn't even notice.

Harrison's head is shrunk between his shoulders. Type "misery" into one of those search engines, his picture will come up.

Poor Kitten's figured out this is serious a little too late.

But my words still taste like ash, and my soul kicks in protest as I say, "We proceed."

I can't say anything else and be me.

9

By the time the ridiculously large twin-rotor Chinook chopper hones in on Chen's beacon, we're ready. I've layered lightweight, flat, flexible pads of foamed metal body armor over my chest, back, and groin, and clipped grenades, extra ammunition clips, and a couple different knives onto my belt.

Methodical preparation completely occupies my mind. I have no thoughts for anything but the task, for survival, for escape.

I keep telling myself that. The mantra fills the rest of my brain.

There's no space whatsoever to pay attention to Kitten.

No, not Kitten. That's too cute.

Harrison.

God, if I called him Kitten on an open mic? A little back-and-forth before a mission is fine, but you don't slag a teammate when weapons are live.

Harrison has nailed his sack back on, at least. His boots are meticulously laced and tied, and his body armor's strapped on properly. We gunbunnies have foamed metal armor, the stuff that stops even armor-piercing rounds, but Harrison's hard, heavy ballistic armor is a few years old.

The sight pisses me off. Yeah, foamed metal's damned expensive, and there's only one company that makes it, and the production line's slower than a crap after eating nothing but pancakes for a month.

But we are professionals, we charge professional rates, and even the kid should get proper protection.

His contract says he won't fight.

He probably didn't know enough to specify that armor in his contract.

Hell, I've seen him fight. If it comes to Kitt—Harrison's fists, the rest of us are already dead. His best chance is to get his hands up and hope the Ecuadoran troops don't toss him in a pit full of those snakes with the venom that makes you swell up until you pop.

The sight of him tightening the last shoulder strap still pisses me off, though.

The chopper's getting closer. In another few seconds, nobody'll be able to hear anything but its roar and the wash.

I reach up to grab Kitten's armored shoulder.

He jumps.

Way too high-strung.

Even through the layers of armor and my skin-tight flexible synthetic leather gloves, though, his warmth seems to seep through to my hand.

It's so annoying I almost want to yank him to the ground, but instead I tug the shoulder until he gets the idea a second later. Leaning close to his ear, I bellow over the approaching machine's throbbing roar. "Stay behind someone! Keep in the middle!"

He nods.

I let him go.

My hand retains his imaginary warmth the whole time we're being winched up through the night into the chopper. The pilot's flunky has barely slammed the big door shut when we're rocketing southwest over the mountains.

The Chinook's quieter than you might expect, but it's still a cargo model. I greet the noise-cancelling helmet like a gut-shot man welcomes morphine.

I only get a moment of blessed silence when Chen says, "Comms check."

"Bradley," I say.

"Tarmack."

"Harrison." Kitten sounds collected. Good.

"Shelley."

"Broadwell." He's got no drawl at all now.

I settle on one of the cargo helicopter's narrow aluminum benches. I always thought choppers shook fiercely, but next to an earthquake this Chinook's a massage chair. Kitten—dammit, *Harrison*, settles down opposite me. He looks almost peaceful now, breathing deeply with his eyes closed.

It's like he's realized that he's strapped into the ride, and there's no getting off now, so he might as well focus on it.

His chest plate shifts when he inhales.

Dammit, I'm imagining his chest now. Those firm, taut cross-trainer muscles, flexing and relaxing beneath the armor.

Muscles? If I want big muscles, all I have to do is strip and look in the mirror.

I have *got* to get my head in the game, or Harrison's dead.

I mean, I'm dead.

Shit.

I'm dead.

10

Sliding beneath us at a hundred-some miles an hour, Guayaquil at midnight is a ruined tapestry of flickering lights. Someone's built a bonfire at the soccer stadium, creating a little oval pool of light. A string of working street lights runs down one of the main freeways like a strand of Christmas lights, brilliant white against the tiny amber/yellow fires here and there. A broad swath of cinders marks the remnants of a firestorm on the western arm of the bay, a malignant red radiance cremating who knows how many homes, dreams, and lives.

To the south and west, the implacable Pacific swallows those lights, returning only the feeble reflection of the sinking sliver of moon.

Even way up here, the stink of ash fills the chopper.

And while a Chinook's aluminum bench seat might seem a massage chair after an earthquake, massage chairs have cushions. My butt… does not.

My teammates have all made their own accommodations with the chopper's vibration. Even Harrison—not Kitten, that's right—has propped himself in a corner. Every few minutes, I watch him shift his weight from one glute to the other, keeping the blood flowing.

No, I am not watching him. He's just… sitting across from me. A little to the side. Pretty much straight across.

Sort of.

I'm yelling at myself inside my own skull, cursing my stupidity by working through my collection of Finnish obscenities, when Chen's voice on my radio breaks our silence. "Attention, please."

I straighten my neck to show willing.

"With Klaver's loss, we must rearrange teams."

I'm glad to hear that. Klaver and I were on the processing plant detail, planting enough incendiaries to make sure the place burned down to the concrete. You need one person to do the wiring, and at least one more to watch that person's back.

"Shelley and Tarmack, you will handle the processing plant."

As Shelley and Tarmack acknowledge I'm thinking: me and Broadwell, me and Chen, just not—

Chen says, "Broadwell and I will take the administrative center."

Fuck.

"Bradley, can you protect Harrison in the data center?"

I take a breath and key my mike. "Yes."

Harrison's voice shakes a little. "Acknowledged."

Chen continues, "We'll go lights out in a couple minutes, right before we begin our descent. Last chance for any personal requirements."

Harrison settles back against the strut.

I key my mike. "Hey, Harrison. Go piss."

He sits up. Those lips are pursed in surprise. His mouth moves, but I hear nothing.

"Your mike, kid."

He pushes the button. "Excuse me?"

"Once we get the van on the road, it ain't stopping. And if you piss your pants, you aren't getting back in my van."

He's pissed, all right.

But if things go wrong, if he comes under fire for the first time… well, let's just say I know *extremely* well exactly what good advice I've just given him.

Advice. Instruction. Whatever.

That jaw tightens. His damn dimple actually flashes in the stark light. Face the color of a ripe McIntosh apple, he stands and makes his way forward to the WC.

Tarmack's laughing, and even Shelley's cracked a smile.

My earpiece clicks again. "Private channel," Chen says.

I nod.

"I'm concerned about Harrison," Chen says.

I am, too.

But not in the right way.

"You've been able to keep him in line. Do you believe you can continue to do so?"

I key my mike. "Yes."

"Good." Chen pauses. "You are authorized to use any level of force necessary to make him complete his task. Do you understand?"

The words hit me like a bullet to the gut.

Chen's telling me to scruff Kitten and drag him along if I must.

Or shoot him—say, in the leg.

My hands brushed his thigh once, when I was throwing him around and did a nice easy double-leg take-down. And with the knee pick. And the single leg, actually.

Now that I think about it, Kitten has really nice legs. Hard, but flexible.

He quivered when I grabbed him that first time, right before I blew him off his feet.

The thought of putting a bullet in any of that sickens me.

At my brief pause, Chen says, "I do not like this order. I do not give it lightly. But if the computer center survives, or if we're forced to destroy it by more conventional means, our mission fails. And Klaver was his backup."

I want to puke.

Or, so help me—cry.

Actually fucking cry.

Kitten does not belong here.

And if he gets sick or wanders off, I get to take him out behind the barn and shoot him.

Maybe I can… what? *Charm* the kid? Make kissy faces and cooing noises?

I key my mike.

"Understood."

11

I don't *know* why this specific contract exists. And why we have these specific targets in this site.

But let's play Very Experienced Guess.

Any guess starts with the facts. I read the *Washington Post* every day, so: here's what we know:

Two weeks ago, Ecuador's latest national election kicked in. The center-right party slunk out, the center-left swaggered in. New majority in the only legislative house. Promises of big changes and major new legislation to make everyone's life better.

You know, the usual fertilizer.

Five days ago, the new government sent soldiers into this food processing plant owned by a Chinese-backed mega-corp, a couple dozen miles south of Guayaquil. The whole staff, from accountants to shrimp deveiners, got searched on their way out—thoroughly searched. Yeah, like that. Staff kept their wallets and every peso (or whatever the hell they use here), but not one piece of paper or digital device. No flash drives, even.

The new Ecuadoran chief put out a call for all sorts of inspectors and researchers.

About three hours after that, Chen called me. The gig's not easy, but straightforward.

A fire in Processing Shed Four. There's a tank of some nasty flammable chemical in there, because what's fresh shrimp without a healthy layer of preservative? Keeps the vitamins in, you know. Urge the fire along, reduce the place to concrete and ash.

Another fire in the administrative building, near the front gate. Obviously caused by drifting cinders from Shed Four.

The computer center, at the back of the whole place? A firmware virus, to make every hard drive shake, spin, and shred itself. That's suspicious, but: you threw the whole IT staff out! A virus got in, and there wasn't anybody here to stop it.

That's what I *know*.

Now, let's speculate.

When a government changes, it takes a while for business folks to figure out how to get bribe money into the right hands. You can't just walk up to El Presidente and say, "Hey, you want a new Jag? Or would a Rolls be more your taste? Red or black?" Not in a democracy, at least.

Sometimes, the bribe money isn't enough. The government slows down permits, an official shows up with blank paperwork and a big sack, life goes on.

But if the new guys have found something really juicy, something that taints the other guys so badly that exposing it will keep them out of office for a generation, something that makes Big Foreign Company look utterly foul, then you take the bribes and bring the hammer down anyway.

We're here to get rid of the evidence.

We can't just blow up the whole place. It's basically a square, about a mile on a side. That's a whole lot of plastique. You can't fake that as a natural disaster, unless you've got an earthquake stashed in your back pocket. Plus, there's no way to claim it's an accident, or thieves, or terrorists from Uruguay or the States or Brazil or whoever the Ecuadoran press gets their people riled up at these days.

Who's the customer? Probably the opposition party. Maybe the mega-corp, if it's *really* damning. No, not human rights damning, more like "Tay-Stee Shrimp Spread is made of people and puppies" damning.

Maybe the earthquake already did our job. No way to tell without going in.

But the earthquake's a great excuse. A fire is suspicious, but when the Andes shrug and half the city's burned to cinders? El Presidente curses his luck and falls back on traditional blackmail and thuggery.

As we get closer to the plant, the pilot douses the running lights. If there's any troops left there, no need to shine bright lights to announce our presence. Presumably they don't have radar gear—they would have relied on the Guayaquil airport, and that's just flat-out gone.

So they'll hear the chopper get close. Really close.

It'll hit the ground.

We shoot out: a minivan for me and Kitten, motorbikes for the others. All electric, so they run silent. We'd planned to throw the gear in the van and escape during the chaos of the burning buildings, leaving everyone unsure if we'd been there at all.

The chopper will bounce up right away, like a high-bounce ball, vanishing before anyone can investigate.

Now? Who knows if there's any soldiers left, or if the processing shed's fallen into the Pacific, or if a busted natural gas line has caused the fire for us. Any of that, we claim the credit and cash the check.

Or maybe the earthquake's damaged every scrap of infrastructure, and setting the fire will trigger a conflagration and burn everything down.

Our heirs will collect our checks.

I've left part of mine to my folks—they did the best they could with a daughter born King of the Dwarves, I want them taken care of—but mostly, it goes to the Saratoga, New York Humane Society.

Oh, shut up.

The aluminum seat has just about vibrated its way up to my kidneys when Chen's voice comes over the headset again. "Infra-red shows the compound is intact but without power. We've identified a cluster of soldiers, perhaps a dozen, at the front gate, but no other targets. Minor damage to the buildings. We will set down at the tertiary location. It's time."

My brain flips through the memorized map. We'll be near the processing plant. The HQ team will go one way, Kitten and I the other. We get the long drive, but we have the nicest ride.

"There's road damage," Chen continues, "but escape plan three appears feasible."

Plan three: get a few miles away, ditch the gear, and shift to Bewildered Tourist.

The van's clamped by the Chinook's cargo ramp, right behind the electric bikes. I claim the wheel, cranking the seat all the way up and as far forward as it can go. Kitten straps himself into the passenger seat like he's in a funhouse ride, which this kind of is.

Except it's a ride that might get him killed.

One of the important principles of freelancing is that you've got to look after yourself first. There's no point in running through the fire zone to help a teammate only to catch a bullet in the spine. People want to help each other, but I've worked hard to beat that instinct down.

But looking at his tall form, strapped in the seat, trying to be brave, it's pretty clear that my instincts have come kicking back full strength.

And those instincts run smack against my training and habits.

I've got to treat this whole mission like I'm brand new. Watch myself. Think clearly.

It's the best way I can keep Kitten alive.

The Chinook's interior lights go out.

My stomach rolls and the Chinook drops.

We swap the noise-dampening helmets for radio earpieces and night vision goggles.

Moments later, the ramp lowers.

The pilot's flunky smacks the big button to disengage the clamps holding the bikes and van in place.

Broadwell and Chen roll down on their bikes, with a little hop at the end as they clear the ramp and hit the tarmac.

Shelley and Tarmack follow.

I touch a button on the dash, and the electric minivan rolls into the night.

12

The fancy night vision goggles turn the scene to lurid greens and reds.

The biggest source of light is the Chinook, barely waiting for the van's rear bumper to clear the ramp before ascending into the sky. The tarmac-covered ground is a cool dim blue, with crazy cracks of pure black zigzagging across it. The earthquake's hit here too, but the surface doesn't look too treacherous. We'll want to go slowly, in case there's sinkholes or just tire-eaters.

A building rises beside us, glowing pink with just a little of the day's retained heat.

Best of all, the vibration's gone. But it's replaced with—

"Oh my God," Harrison says. "What is that smell?"

"Dead cows," I say. "Probably a couple dismantled whales. A metric shitload of bad bananas. It's a food processing plant." I make myself sound a heck of a lot better than that gut-punching stink makes me feel. "Lighten up, kitten. This is where you *earn* that fat paycheck."

"Right." Mentioning our pay perks him up more than anything else I say. That chin rises as he studies the asphalt plain.

So the kitten's greedy? The thought does more to cool the confusing burble in my soul than anything I've told myself. He looks too good. Fucker *smells* too good. But greed… it brings him down with the rest of us.

Makes him mortal.

Kitten's just another one of us, I tell myself. He's taking ridiculous risks, for a pile of cash. Give him another year, and he'll be in the ground or have all that pretty boy charm scraped off. Probably a big scar across his face or something.

And maybe I can use that greed to keep him going. Keep from putting a bullet in him.

That perfection's going to get knocked around.

But I don't want to be the one to do it.

Ahead of us, the lithe heat-red form of Chen is already kicking his bike forward, with Broadwell in his shadow. The chopper's already far enough up that I should be able to hear the bike motors, but the electrics glide freakishly silent towards the administrative center.

What's the point of a big bike if it doesn't have a little roar and rattle?

Shelley and Tarmack aim their bikes towards the side door of the processing shed. This building is their destination, and they're close enough to walk—but they want the bikes right by the door and ready to go. When they come out, they'll be in a *real* hurry.

I roll my neck to loosen the knots and punch the starter.

With the chopper gone, the only sound is the chirping and scraping of the billions of bugs bouncing off the windscreen.

Kitten's head is swiveling like an owl's, trying to see everywhere simultaneously. It's better than him being buried in a cellphone right now, but he's way too keyed up.

"Chill, Harrison," I say.

"We're on," he says.

"With night vision, you don't pick things out of the background," I say. "People, cars, all that shows up pink and red. We'll see them well before they're close enough to do anything. But the only red I see is your head bouncing around like it's on a spring. And you're burning all your adrenalin now, when you just might need it later." It'd be easier if I could just choke Kitten out, slap him awake when we get to the data center. Plus, it'd be an excuse to hold him again—

No, no, *hell* no.

I try to steady myself with a breath. My friend Beaks tells me all the time to breathe before I decide someone needs a good swift kick to the head.

"Look out the side," I say. "I've got the rest."

My earpiece clicks. Tarmack says, "Target one entered."

We dropped Tarmack and Shelley right at their building. They better be the first in. I try being annoyed at them, hoping to distract myself from Kitten.

Kitten's heat seeps between the plates of his body armor. He's an inferno over there, his warmth spilling over.

The van bumps and lurches as we cross a crumpled bump of asphalt.

Kitten lets out this little meep of surprise.

I wrench my attention back to the road. Focus!

In a couple minutes we're going down this little two-lane path between a metal warehouse and giant tanks, like tuna cans fed stupid amounts of growth hormone. I'm keeping my eyes on the road in front of us, sparing quick glances to the side, but there's no heat.

The van hits a rough patch of road and starts to vibrate.

I clench the wheel tighter and ease off the accelerator.

We're slowing—but the vibration's getting worse.

Dread seeps from my gut.

Fresh black crazed cracks appear in the road before us.

The van's really shaking now. And there's a growing bone-deep rumble that doesn't come through my ears, but through my feet and my seat.

"Oh, shit," Kitten says.

13

With the ground coming apart beneath us, I stomp on the accelerator.

The van surges forward.

Those looming tanks right next to us—what're they full of? Acid? Chlorine? What if one's full of bleach, and the one next to it ammonia? Or some evil shit that will catch fire the second it hits air?

Can't drive through the four-story warehouse on the other side.

The only way out is forward.

Kitten grabs the Jesus bar but doesn't say anything, just hangs on for dear life and braces his feet against the footboards. Good—I don't need to be petting his fur to soothe him, the earth itself is trying to kill us.

I'd feel better if the van made some noise too, if I could feel it roar back—but the electric motor stays silent. Not that a V-8 would punch through the furious stone beneath us.

Forget the tanks—we're a quarter mile from the Pacific Ocean.

The van's slewing sideways, like we're hydroplaning. I turn into the spin, trying to bring it under control the way you do on an icy road, but it's just not helping.

It's worse than last time. The steering wheel feels like it's coming apart in my hands, my iron grip dissolving. Something crashes onto the roof and bounces away, and the windshield faces a wall of pipes, but it doesn't matter because the van's moving sideways even though my foot's not on the pedal or on anything at all and the seat belt's vibrating into me like a saw making my teeth shudder in their sockets.

My insides are dissolving too.

I'm coming apart.

There's a sudden sickening plunge.

I glimpse a tank wall shredding like cake.

A wall of broken earth shoots up in front of us—yards away? Miles? Who knows?

I don't know how, but even through the world's violated screaming I hear Kitten scream.

And I need him again.

That's worse than last time, too.

The world's coming apart, and I'm utterly alone.

I'm going to die alone.

I've always known I'm going to die. One day a plan will fail, or a goon will get lucky, or I'll screw up. Or I'll keep working when my reflexes slow, when my muscles get weak, when I'm past my sell-by date, because I'm too damn stupid to do anything else. Someone will pry my gun from my hand and carry on. I'll be cremated in a burning building. My teammates on that mission, and from a whole bunch of other jobs, will have a drink in my honor. Some will get totally hammered.

And that'll be that.

I remember teasing in preschool.

Kindergarten only got worse, and every year after that.

Dad once told me, after he'd had a couple beers, that when I was still in diapers he stopped taking me to the park because people kept asking him what was wrong with me and the cops told him that if he decked anyone else they'd charge him with felony assault.

Learning to bite back the tears. Learning to not give a fuck what anybody thought.

To defend myself. Not just to fight, but to utterly crush anyone who dared taunt, until nobody dared and they left me alone.

Give me a sneer, and I'll take a tooth.

Even the goddamn military rejected me—not because I was out of shape, not because I couldn't follow orders, not because I'm stupid, but just because I'm too short to be so heavy, so strong.

I got my dream crushed because they wouldn't make a fucking uniform to fit me.

So I found a teacher.

But now—it's like the goddamn Earth is rejecting me. Putting its thumb down. *What have we got here? I thought I got rid of all the Neanderthals thirty thousand years ago? Gimme a second, let me put my thumb down and crush this monster before it does something terrible, like find joy or love, or God forbid, breed. There, that's better, isn't it?*

Breed? Wait—what?

But just once, I want to be held.

Not just by anyone, either.

I want Kitten to hold me.

Maybe… more?

The Earth brings its thumb down.

14

Barely stirring towards consciousness, I taste my lower lip.

Banana?

Fiendishly sweet, disgustingly strong banana. Frankenstein's banana, a mutant Godzilla banana. Something that King Kong would look at and say, "maybe not."

My eyes open gummily.

Complete blackness.

I'm lying on an irregular, vaguely flat surface. It's like a bunch of shipping crates?

I twitch my hand.

It still works.

My fingers find the textured hard plastic surface beneath me. At each touch, they don't want to come away; the skin of my fingertips seize the surface, and I have to tug to peel them away.

Sticky. The cases are sticky.

Fumbling, I find the edge, and trail along it to find a corner capped in hard aluminum.

Equipment cases.

The back of the van had equipment cases.

That's a start.

Another point: I hurt.

Experience tells me I've been hurt a lot worse before. I've been shot, dumped out of a moving train down a steep grassy hill, dumped out of a moving car onto the freeway in LA—fortunately it was just short of rush hour, so we were doing maybe twenty, but still—and don't ask me about that thing with the bulldozer. Seriously, don't ask.

I'm battered and bruised, but nothing feels broken.

But inside my head, I add *ridden in a tumble dryer* to the list.

And I'm sticky.

The cases aren't sticking to my fingers. My fingers are sticking to each other, to the cases, to my clothes, to damn near everything.

What the hell?

I groan and raise my hand, wanting to hold my aching forehead.

"Ma'am!"

Kitten's alive.

I'm surrounded in darkness, battered and bruised, hands sticky and my mouth full of Satan's Private Label banana topping. But hearing Kitten's voice, even if he's calling me ma'am, ignites a fire in my soul and spreads a soothing warmth through my aches.

He's better than ibuprofen.

Maybe not Norco.

I'd like a Norco.

"Kitten," I say. I work my mouth, trying to loosen my jaw. "Situation?"

"Normal," he says with half a laugh. "All *totally* fucked up."

The should worry me.

Instead, his laugh brightens that secret warmth.

Yes, it's a secret warmth. It's got to be secret.

I am not going to make Kitten laugh in my face.

Not after the fucking *planet's* tried to crush me.

I get the hint, okay?

I take a deep breath. Yep, my ribs are fine. I'm still utterly indestructible by any conventional means. "Would you perhaps, just maybe, care to be just a little more specific?"

"Sorry, ma'am." I hear Kitten take his own deep breath. Now that we're deep in the latrine with a fresh load coming down, he's doing a decent job of holding himself together. "I think we're underground."

I like hearing Kitten's voice. I mean, I *really* like hearing him speak.

But his words pour cold dread into my soul.

"The van is sideways," he says. "I broke out a back window, but there's rock on the other side. A metal pipe came through the windshield, it's leaking fruit syrup."

"Tell me the van's not filling up with that shit," I say.

"No, it's running out the passenger window, that's what's on the bottom. It's busted out, seems to be going away all right. There's a few sparks down there in infrared."

"Your goggles work? Good, that's something."

"The radio doesn't," he says. "It clicks, but nobody answers."

Well, shit.

The radio's not meant to work through dirt and stone.

Or maybe we're the only ones left.

"You were out," Kitten says. "I got back here, straightened out some equipment cases to put you on, got you out of your seat. IR said you weren't bleeding, and nothing looked broken, so…" His voice trailed off. "I just raised your feet and hoped."

My feet are raised. And there's something soft under my head, too.

My hair's matted to my head with banana syrup.

And that shit's not just on my head and my hands. Raising my hand to probe for the ceiling, I feel my back tug at the plastic.

I'm utterly covered in banana syrup.

"There's room overhead," Kitten says. "If you swing your feet left, you can sit up proper like."

Hand still raised like an antenna, I hoist myself upright. My brain wobbles in its own juices for a moment, then steadies. The total darkness is disorienting, and the stickiness makes it worse. Shifting one joint at a time, checking for any strains or pains, I swing my feet over until I can sit upright and breathe more easily.

But we're still in darkness.

"Hoping was enough," I say. "Good job."

More than a good job, really.

The darkness really is all-engulfing. Somehow Kitten—*Harrison* had gotten his brain together, escaped the syrup flood—without sight, because those digital lenses don't work when you drench them in goo, and if we're underground there's no heat sources except us. He'd made a pallet for an injured teammate, gotten me—and I'm not a lightweight, not even close—into it, assessed my injuries in the dark and through foamed metal body armor, found a pair of goggles that weren't drenched in banana, and assessed our situation while waiting for me to regain consciousness.

Or die.

Yeah, that.

Sometimes, a good shock that knocks you out sucks out the memories of what happened right before the fade-to-black. Those thoughts never make it into long-term storage. I've teased more than one teammate about how they'd finally admitted their lifelong yearning to be a ballet dancer or a priest right before they blacked out.

I wasn't that lucky.

Sitting here in the dark, though, with only Kitten's rich voice for company, those earthquake realizations echo through me.

All of those years of rejecting rejection?

Useless.

Standing up for myself? Fighting everything in my way?

No good.

It's not just that I don't want to die alone. I don't want to live alone, either.

I want someone who won't look at me and turn away. Or have that flash of *what the fuck* and get all kind and solicitous.

Surrounded in the darkness, I have a sudden flash of light.

Kitten never looked at me like that.

When Kitten first saw me he said "ma'am," like he'd been raised politely, or those Marine manners lessons had taken root.

Some people don't react badly to me—but I can tell.

You just know when someone's disciplining their face.

Freelancers don't care so much. Every one of us is a freak. My buddy Beaks, she's like six foot forty, we've worked together a couple times. After each mission, we go out for the best meal we can get. I thank her for keeping her head up so the opposition has something to shoot at. She asks me to walk under the car and look up to check the trans before we leave. It's okay. Tarmack, he's so damn ugly that he makes me look like a model, and you can bet we go back and forth too.

The people who have earned the right to call me names know who they are.

But I'd never gotten the sense from Kitten that he even had to try.

Okay, so he needed to learn to shut up.

Thinking back, I might have been a little mouthy before my first mission too.

Kitten… is not a complete idiot.

Green as lettuce, sure.

"Okay," I say. "Give me the goggles, let me have a look."

"One thing first," he says. I hear something splash. "Hold out your hand."

I raise a hand, palm up.

Something cool and wet splots across it.

I jump a little, then quickly realize what it is.

Wet cloth.

"I worked like a dog getting these goggles clean," he says. I'm already raising the cloth to my face and scrubbing as he says, "You are not getting them all sticky again."

Cold water isn't the best way to clean syrup. We need about a gallon of soap and a hot tub. But it'll help.

I scrub my hands and bare forearms with the thin, wet wad, then attack my face. The cloth is wet, but it's still imbued with this oddly familiar spicy-sweet aroma completely unlike the horrible banana stink tainting everything. It smells satisfying. Comfortable.

I'm scrubbing my mouth when I realize where I've smelled it before.

It's Kitten's smell.

I'm scrubbing my face with his shirt.

I jerk it away from my mouth. What did I expect? We didn't pack towels for this trip to the seaside.

But on top of my earlier revelations, it's just a bit much for me. I hold out a hand. "Goggles."

In the deep silence of the earth, there's the click of a buckle and the sound of leather sliding against itself. Holding my hand out in the darkness feels stupid, but less stupid than holding his shirt in the other.

It's not that I'm reluctant to let it go. I just… don't want to lose my washrag in the dark.

A moment later, the blade edge of his hand, the side with the pinky, brushes my bare forearm.

I jump a little at the contact.

"There you are," he says.

His hand turns so he can lay his fingers on my arm. "I do *not* want to drop these."

"Fine," I say. His fingers are wired with one-ten volts. If my hair wasn't soaked in banana syrup, it would be standing on end.

He's not being creepy. Not doing the Asshole Handbook's gentle touch to get a woman accustomed to his presence. It takes him maybe a second to find my hand.

It's the longest second of my life.

Even longer than the thing with the bulldozer.

The rest of my arm aches, but not where he touches me.

Where he touches me, I only feel that tingle.

His hand finds mine. Cups the back of it, without pressure.

His hands are bigger than mine.

That's not a surprise—it's my frame that's huge, I'm not like Mister Potato Head.

But his hand around mine makes me feel—safe?

What the hell is this? We are *buried alive*, and Kitten holding my hand makes me feel like a baby in my mother's arms?

No, it's not like being a baby.

Not like that at *all*.

It runs deeper than that, sending that quiver back up my torso, triggering sparks that I really don't want to think about.

My every instinct says to yank my hand away.

But he's found my hand to give me the goggles.

If we're going to live, I have to endure that gentle touch.

No, *this* is the longest second of my life.

But then cold hard plastic presses into my hand.

I close my fingers. "Got them."

He pulls his hand back right away.

My spirits plunge like I've been marooned on the far side of the moon.

The goggles are still sticky, but I can tell he's done a bunch of work on them. The strap is sticky, but so is the back of my head, so I slip them on.

The first thing I see is Kitten, gleaming bright by infrared.

He's taken most his clothes off.

15

Where did I think the T-shirt came from, anyway? Kitten didn't pack his shaving kit and a couple changes of clothes. That sort of thing was waiting for us in a safe house in Guayaquil—in the part that was a lake of cinders, I think.

"Everything was sticky," Kitten says.

He's sitting on an upended equipment case, facing me. I instinctively look to see if he's wearing underwear—yes, I've seen naked men before, but I've always had a bit of warning when the facilities were that primitive.

Actually, he's wearing pants. Boots, too.

Part of me's disappointed.

But in infrared, his muscle definition is just amazing.

The heat-sensitive goggles, even with banana-smeary lenses, show how his blood flows through every strong, flexible curve of muscle.

Lifting weights is one thing. Any moron can pick up heavy things over and over again. Many morons do exactly that. But Kitten's paid proper attention to the different muscle groups, and done enough stretching that everything can still bend nicely.

My face is flushing so hot that I'm sure he can see me even without infrared. But his eyes are a little to my left, like he's trying to figure out where my head is based on where he found my hand.

I need to think of something else.

He stretches? My girl Beaks stretches too. Maybe I should introduce—

Hell no, my brainstem screams. Beaks can find her own, she *has* her own, I'm keeping this one.

Well, that wasn't helpful.

I make my voice hard. "Stay right there."

Kitten puts his hands on his thighs, palms up.

Even through the tough khaki pants, the infrared displays the smooth contours of his thighs and calves.

"Right," I say, putting Kitten's wet shirt on an equipment case and looking away. "Let's see what we've got."

The van is a shambles.

The van's lying on the passenger side, with the nose slightly down. We're sitting near the rear doors. The warmth from our bodies is enough to cast a little heat, making the half dozen disarrayed equipment cases vague but discernable. They all tumbled when the van tipped, and Kitten only straightened enough to lie me on.

The front of the van is a cold, black, mess. I need a moment to figure out what the faint shadows I can perceive mean.

That long dim shape, with the rounded end? That must be the pipe Kitten mentioned. It's hanging about a foot into the passenger compartment, constantly oozing pitch-black turgid syrup. The end is pinched almost shut, like the pipe was wrenched until it busted halfway.

I crawl forward on hands and knees, over sticky unstable equipment cases.

The van itself doesn't even twitch, though.

We're pinned in here pretty good.

I stick my head next to the syrup pipe, careful not to touch it. Just crawling here has gotten my hands sticky again, but that doesn't mean I want the Banana Puke hair treatment.

The driver's side window is busted out. I can see the broken edges of glass.

Beyond that?

Cold, untextured darkness.

I look down.

The syrup swallows everything.

I study the equipment cases. There, that one will do. "Opening a case," I say.

"Okay," Kitten says. He's holding himself still, trying not to panic in the darkness and doing a decent job of it so far. I'll have to give him a turn on the goggles—only a few moments of vision have soothed me a lot.

Helps that there's something nice to look at.

I snap open the rifle case. We didn't expect to need rifles, but Chen packed a couple of AK-74s. They're the lowest common denominator of rifles these days, with all the accuracy of flung dog shit, but I don't care about their accuracy.

They're the closest thing I have to a long stick.

I jab the barrel upwards, out the driver's side window.

It goes about six inches and hits something solid.

Dirt patters down.

Shit.

I climb down and check the bottom, out the passenger window.

The barrel sinks six inches into the syrup before hitting something.

I jab it around, but no: no way through there.

I retract the sticky barrel. "Breaking glass," I say.

"Thanks for the warning," he says.

I reverse the rifle and attack the busted windshield with the butt.

The syrup pipe did the hard part for me. I just have to finish knocking the glass out of the frame.

And beyond?

More dirt.

A few more pipes.

I can get the rifle barrel into a hole, and plunge it all the way in—but it's only about a foot wide. If I grab Kitten and wad him up *really* tight, I can probably just barely squeeze him through there.

That's not how I want to squeeze him.

Keep my mind on the job. Keep my mind on the job.

It's maybe another fifteen minutes before I admit defeat and crawl back towards Kitten. I'm sweating freely, and it's a relief to plant my butt on a crate.

Kitten's not looking well. His face has lost some of his color, and I see his lips move. Multiplication tables, maybe? Something to keep his mind on.

I need a rest, and he could use a break. "Here," I say, pulling the goggles off my head.

Darkness plunges around me. I keep my eyes closed—it's easier to pretend that I'm playing a game than stare into the blackness. I don't reach for Kitten's hand, instead fumbling the glasses out towards his thigh.

I hit something that gives just a little, and freeze.

A breath later, Kitten's hand brushes mine again.

He is so damn warm.

"Got them," he says.

"Good," I say. "See if you can find the flares."

I hear his breath stop. "Flares?"

"You know. Flares. They do have flares in the Marines, right? Even if you're a computer feeder?"

"Yeah, but…"

The worry in his voice tears at me. If I reached out to give him a hug right now, he'd probably grab hold of me.

To be fair, I'm pretty terrified myself.

"That's concentrated syrup. It's maybe ninety percent sugar."

"So?"

"It burns."

16

I can't help imagining the van exploding into flames.

The heat would plow through here like a chimney.

"Okay," I say slowly. "You're sure on that?"

"I have half my chemistry degree," Kitten says. "It's hard to get started, but you light one of those magnesium flares, it'll burn like crazy."

The van's felt small all along—but now it's utterly claustrophobic. My heart's pounding, and my blood's shuddering with it. The stink of bananas, already unbearably thick, seems to squeeze itself further down my throat.

If I get out of here, I'm never eating bananas again.

I need a moment to quell the rush of fear. When I don't answer him, Kitten starts talking.

"The syrup is going somewhere, and it's not getting caught by air pressure, there's a way for air to get down here. All we need is light. We're about an hour and forty minutes from sunrise. If the air's coming down here, maybe the light can too. We don't need much, even just a reflection to make the goggles work."

"I checked," I say. "There's no way out."

"How did you check?"

"Poked around with a rifle."

"Give us some light," he says, "and we might—just might—see something, ma'am."

"Oh, for fuck's sake," I snarl. "We are buried alive under who knows how much rock and dirt and buildings and shit. Call me Bradley."

Kitten gives this little snort. "Sure… Bradley."

"What's so funny about that?" I demand.

"My best friend from back in high school is named Bradley. He's got a gut like a hippo and wears glasses so thick you could use them to start fires."

"He's that big at your age?" I say.

"No, that was in high school." Kitten's voice turns dry. "You should see him now."

I give a little laugh. It's not funny, but right now, it's the best we're going to have.

"Nice guy, though," he says. "So, Bradley's fine with me."

He says my name slowly, with two distinct syllables, like he enjoys the way it tastes.

I need to stop thinking that way, *right* now.

"I'm not having you think of me as a fat guy in glasses," I say. "My first name's Liza."

"Liza?" Kitten says that slowly too, goddammit. "As in Elizabeth?"

"You ever say that *filthy* word in reference to me," I say, "and I will drown you face-down and ass-deep in banana syrup."

I can hear his smile. "Yes, ma'am Liza."

We're silent for a moment.

"You've thought this through," I say.

"Not much else to do. You weren't up for cribbage."

I can't find a fault in his logic, but I absolutely *hate* waiting. "You're saying we sit here until dawn?"

"A little after. Give the sun time to get over the mountains."

"How do you know how long it is till dawn, anyway?"

"I've got a great time sense," Kitten says. "If I'd been knocked out I'd have no clue. I've gotta look at a clock in the morning when I wake up, but once I set my timer I'm good."

I'm tired. I ache, everywhere. "Okay."

Worse, my soul is having its own storm.

We're the only people in the world, again.

No, I'm not risking rejection again.

I try to relax.

The darkness folds itself around me.

I'm getting colder.

I'm terrible at waiting. Give me a countdown timer, and I can chant with it until go time. If there's nothing to do, let me go. But this sitting in the darkness, with nothing but my own unruly feelings for company, is pure punishment.

I could go sit next to Kitten.

I bet he's shivering too.

Finally I say, "K—Harrison."

"Yeah?"

"You did your time in the service. You have half a chemistry degree, I'm guessing with benefits. Computer skills. Put on a suit, you could get a job anywhere."

"I've got one. Had one."

"So why are you here? Don't mistake me," I say hurriedly, "I'm glad I'm not stuck in this hole by myself." And being stuck two feet from you hovers in this weird place between joy and torture. "But why would you sign up for a freelance job?"

He sighs. "Long story, Liza."

"I know we have to get to the party soon, but I'm willing to be late."

Kitten doesn't have to tell me. He's low man on the totem pole, but this isn't mission-related.

But he's probably just as lonely and scared as I am, if not nearly so conflicted.

I hear him take a deep breath and let it out. "Fine. I did my time, got my honorable discharge. This guy found me my first night of freedom, gives me a card."

"I probably know the guy," I say. "He called it short-term work?"

"I tell him I'm not interested, but he tells me to keep it. If I stay in shape, and I need money in a hurry, he can help me out. He splits, but…" Kitten takes a deep breath. "I keep the card, because you never know. And I start at Michigan State."

My stomach's got this sick knot.

I don't know what's coming.

But whatever made a clean-cut college kid sign up for this shit life can't be nice.

"My mom got sick last month," Kitten says. "Cancer."

"That's pretty shitty," I say, sincerely.

"It's operable, though? If they get it within a couple months. And if you have insurance."

My stomach drops out. "And she doesn't."

"I've got two younger brothers, a younger sister. She's twelve." Kitten's voice catches a little. "I don't want her growing up without a mom."

I don't trust my own feelings, my own thoughts, my own decisions.

But I'm a human being.

And there's only one human thing to do right now.

I fumble out in the dark.

The back of my hand touches a cloth-covered, syrup-soaked knee.

A second later his hand is on mine.

I grab hold, not too tight.

His fingers clasp mine.

Kitten's palm is as large as mine, but his fingers are longer, more sensitive. There's not an ounce of thug in him.

My skin sizzles at his touch.

And he's not letting go.

17

The darkness isn't so oppressive now. Kitten's hand warms mine. That heat slithers up my arm, leaving a trail of sparks.

I ache to see his handsome face, those crystal blue eyes, even that damned dimple in his chin.

But if the lights were on, he wouldn't want to look at me.

Kitten takes a shuddering breath. "The paycheck for this, it's enough to get Mom her surgery, get the Horde started on college. Heck, now that Kelly's out of the picture, I'll have more than enough."

"Kelly?" I ask.

"My girl."

Bright jealousy flashes through me.

"Ex-girl," he says. "Mom got sick, and Kelly's high maintenance. I think I learned my lesson there."

The jealousy turns to a pattering of my heart and a flicker of hope in my soul.

Goddamn it, my heart does not *patter*. That's a teenage girl thing, and I never really was a teenage girl. I don't *have* a goddamn heart. Not like that.

And hope?

I am *not* going to make this pretty boy spell it out to me.

Kitten has no idea of the storm that's going on inside me. "All I have to do, is get out of here."

I squeeze his hand. "We'll get out. Fire up your gear. Cook those computers."

He squeezes back.

My heart beats more quickly.

"If they're even there," he says. "They might be on the seabed or something."

"We were on our way there," I say. "If the ocean didn't eat us, the datacenter's still there."

"Thanks."

I have my fingers cradled around the blade edge of his hand, my thumb curled beneath his. When his fingers even twitch, I'll let go.

But he seems content to hold my hand.

It's grave dark, and just as claustrophobic. Kitten would probably hold on to Tarmack's hand right now.

Kitten squeezes my hand again. I feel this stab of regret—I want him to be okay down here, sure, but I really don't want him to release my hand.

I loosen my fingers so he can slip free. Holding hands isn't something I can put up a fight over—well no, yes I can put up a fight over holding hands. But I don't want to grapple with Kitten.

Not the way I'd grapple with Tarmack, at least.

Dammit.

"I have to thank you," Kitten says.

I jerk in surprise.

Kitten lets go of my hand.

Stupid fucking gentlemanly behavior! Instinctively, I snatch his fingers out of the darkness.

Kitten lets me take that comfortable grip again.

Once my hand's settled back where it belongs (does not belong, does *not* belong!) I say, "Thank me for what?"

"For throwing me around like a… kitten."

"No," I say, "that was stupid."

His clench on my hand is fierce. "You needed me to pay attention. You told me what I needed to know to stay alive. Yeah, I did basic, I did the morning workout, but then they put me in a computer room. That's not the real thing, not at all. I was…"

His voice trails off.

I gently squeeze his hand.

"I was scared," Kitten says. "Mouthing off. Trying to convince myself I wasn't ready to piss my pants—and yeah, if you hadn't told me that too, we'd be swimming in syrup *and* piss." The smell of his warm breath fills the darkness.

"Well," I smile, "then I've saved us from a fate worse than death."

"I don't know how you keep it together so well," Kitten says.

I can't help laughing—not a chuckle, but a full-on belly laugh. "Keep it together?" My hand squeezes his more tightly, but my free hand folds across my chest plate as if to hold my guts in.

"Yeah," he says.

"Kitten," I say as the laughter fades, "you have no clue just how scared I am right now."

Saying that right now loosens a knot in my heart.

I can't believe how *good* it feels to admit that.

"Maybe we'll get out of here," I say. "Maybe there is an air vent—but it might be only a few inches wide. Maybe wherever that syrup's draining into will fill up. We might both drown in fucking bananas. One more earthquake? An aftershock? We are not only dead, but *flat*."

He squeezes my hand, almost tight enough to hurt.

But the not-pain, the fire that spreads up my arm, gives me the power to continue.

"But you know what I'm really scared of?" The words are exploding out of me now. "I'm scared of living. I mean, dying, sure, I'm ready for that. But living like this? My only friends are gunbunnies and explosive experts and a million kinds of mayhem mechanics."

These feelings have been buried in me for too long—not just since I first saw Kitten, not even since I became a mercenary, but before that, long before that.

I'm fifteen again, another school dance flyer that some fuckwit's scribbled *enjoy your free night!* on it and stuffed into my locker, I'm wadding it up and stuffing it deep in the trash.

I'm twelve, and I've gotten in Mom's makeup, I'm really trying, but I look like a Neolithic Bozo the Clown, and it won't come off, and it won't come off, and Mom finds me and shows me the remover and I want to die.

I'm eight, and there's blood on my knuckles, and I'm trying to decide if I need to kick Jimmy's head, I still remember his name, do I need to kick

him again or has he learned to keep his stupid mouth shut and not call me
a troll, and at the same time I'm twenty-five thinking: stupid kid was just
repeating what his parents said, what all the parents were saying.

My voice is rising now, my feelings detonating with so much pressure
that they're an explosion, the fire in my soul enough to crack the side of the
van and bring the rock down on us and I just can't care about that.

Kitten puts his other hand over mine and squeezes.

Somehow, that gives me the strength to not come completely apart.

"I'm big, yes, and I'm short, and my head is square like a block of
concrete, and nobody's ever going to mistake me for a pretty woman, or
even *a* woman, but goddamn it, there's got to be more to life than just
blowing shit up and killing anyone who's in the way for a fucking paycheck.
It's not supposed to be biggest bank account wins, is it? I've got enough to
buy a whole fucking island and throw everyone else off of it,"

I'm shaking now, and crying dammit, I haven't cried since the last time
I got shot, and I made jokes the whole time, but this hurts worse than a
bullet through the leg.

"For just once in my life," I shout, "is it too much to ask for a little
goddamn motherfucking tenderness?"

And that... is when I attack Kitten.

18

Both his hands surround one of mine.

The poor guy doesn't have a chance.

I tighten my grip, bringing my other hand forward, sliding it up his bare arm, all that syrup-sticky skin over his strength, staying connected just like I've practiced a million times in the dojo, until my fingers brush his chin.

Kitten's holding himself perfectly still, like he doesn't know what's going on.

He really doesn't.

Even if he thinks he knows, he's got no clue.

I grab his chin with one hand.

Twist the clasped hand, so his grip falls away, and bring it up.

I know the shape of his head. I spent enough time looking at it today.

That free hand easily finds his ear, then slips up to grab the strap of the night vision goggles.

He hasn't buckled the goggles on very tightly. Good.

That means they pull off easily.

It's not like he needs that ear, anyway.

That hand slips into the syrup-drenched tangle of his hair. It's okay—the hair is too short to get tangled enough to stop me.

I lunge forward.

My lips crash into his.

When I say "crash," that's exactly what I mean. It's like a car crash.

For a fraction of a fraction of a second, his lips burn against mine. The taste sends lightning through my skull, down my spine, triggering every nerve I have.

But Kitten's mouth is hanging a little bit open, exposing his teeth.

My lower lip gets caught between his teeth and mine.

There's a flash of pain through my lip—not terrible, not even very bad compared to getting shot or electrocuted or thrown out of a moving train.

But it's enough to shock some sense back into me.

Embarrassment floods through me.

No, not embarrassment.

Shame.

What am I going to do, rape him?

I jerk my head back. I'm shaking, everywhere, the trembling in my heart—yes, my heart, I have one of those, I really do, and it's trembling—echoing down my whole body, through my arms, my legs, a cataclysm even worse than the earthquakes.

I've just broken myself.

I've sliced myself open, and everything I've ever smothered, every misbegotten hope and unspeakable dream I've ever choked to death has come oozing out, somehow still alive.

And I'm still crying.

I try to pull away, but Kitten's found his hands now and he's grabbed hold of my arms again.

I know how to break that grip.

I could break it in my sleep.

I don't have the strength.

I need to get away. Crawl up to the front of the van, plunge into the drooling syrup, slither away beneath the earth. Hide. Hide my stupid face forever.

"Hey," Kitten says. "Hey. It's okay, Liza."

"It is not okay!" I scream. "It will *never* be fucking okay!"

He's pulled me close, and I've got to turn my head or I'll smother in his chest, and I can't help grabbing on. I'm sitting on an equipment case and he's sunk to his knees in front of me, holding on like the earth holds the van.

"It's okay," he says over and over again, while I cry myself to pieces.

He strokes my hair. His fingers keep catching in syrupy tangles, but the occasional tug and pull is completely worth it.

Eventually, I stop bawling like a baby.

I sniff. I'm disgusting, my face all covered with snot. And I've gotten it all over Kitten's chest, too.

I pull back, just a little.

Kitten's arms give me an inch. No further. Forget infrared goggles, I can feel his warmth on my tear-swollen face.

There's no tissue, so I wipe my face with the edge of my hand.

"Hang on," Kitten says.

One of his arms releases me. The loss makes me shudder—but I still have one arm.

He shifts his weight a little, like he's lifting a knee in the dark.

"It's wet," he says. "Sorry."

Something cold and clammy touches my shoulder, sucking heat away even in the darkness.

It's Kitten's sadly abused shirt.

I clean my face the best I can.

I've made a sticky mess of Kitten's bare chest as well.

He flinches from the clamminess, but lets me wipe him up a little.

When I move the rag away, he pulls me close again.

I'm too shaken to resist being happy.

Happy?

Yep.

Buried alive, covered in banana sewage, snuggled up with Kitten, I'm happier than I've been since the last time Santa came calling.

He holds me for another moment, subtly rocking me.

Then one of his hands creeps up to cradle the back of my head.

"Liza?" he whispers.

I feel his weight shift in my arms.

He's about to let me go.

I'm grateful. He's not mad at me—hell, Kitten's a good enough man, he signed on as a freelancer just to get enough money to treat his mom's cancer. He probably gets why I snapped. I mean, it's easy enough. He's got eyes, he's got a little sister, he's probably thrilled that little sister doesn't have my fucked-up genes.

But I don't want his arms to move from around me.

His hand cradles the back of my head.

His weight moves again.

I'm practiced martial arts my whole life. I've felt every kind of position change in the world.

But here, engulfed in darkness, I have no idea whatsoever what he is doing.

He's moving wrong.

Aw, shit, did I hurt him? That happens sometimes when I'm upset and everything's gone wrong and I forget just how strong I am.

He's been—no, not kind. Kind is when people look at me and make themselves smile.

He's been... decent? Caring? Trying to help me through this?

If I've hurt him, I am a total shmuck.

His hand shifts from the back of my head.

Then his palm is incredibly warm on my cheek.

And sticky. Banana-sticky.

I instinctively lean into his hand.

It's wonderful.

It's as if Kitten can support my whole head, my whole heart, the whole weight of being Liza Bradley in the palm of one hand.

The darkness has changed, too.

It's warmer.

Right in front of my face.

I quiver.

My breath stops.

Kitten's words come out maybe an inch from my lips.

"This is what tenderness feels like."

His lips barely brush mine.

19

I thought that flash of life when my lips crunched against Kitten's was amazing.

I was wrong.

He's not doing a passionate headbutt. He's staying close, but not jamming himself against me. His lips move freely against mine, their sensitive tissues—muscles—ah, who cares—exploring mine.

If my disastrous attempt was a flash of life, this is like getting plugged directly into the Amazon rainforest.

I'm trembling. Not with exhaustion, like I'd done five, ten, a hundred thousand falls. This is something new. Every nerve is jangling.

I don't think I'm breathing.

He eventually pulls back.

I'm still trembling. My hands are clamped around his back again. I'm squeezing him against the body armor's chest plate, but somehow he can still breathe.

But his lips pulling away from mine leave me devastated.

I have time to think, that's going to have to hold me for a lifetime.

Then he's back.

The part of me that screamed for Kitten's attention, fortunately, gets my lungs to start up again.

But I've got to breathe through my nose.

My lips have never been so busy in my life.

Then there's a weird, moist pressure from his lips.

I jerk in surprise.

Kitten backs off, instantly.

His arms don't even twitch towards letting me go, though.

I need a moment.

Wait—his tongue?

Maybe you kiss someone gently because they're crying. I could accept a pity smooch. I mean, what else could he do?

And I've heard of a pity fuck. I've known a lot of men, that's the only way they get laid.

But I have never imagined, never even conceived, of pity tongue.

Kitten's breath flows warm across my lips, my cheeks.

My lips feel swollen, like I've been punched. And I have, sort of.

But those lips are so sensitive, I can feel him there, through the open air. A millimeter away, maybe.

I grab his head and pull him back.

This time, I open my mouth.

My other hand pulls at his back, drawing him closer, and he tastes incredible, even with the syrup, who gives a shit about the syrup, and I feel his hands scrabbling at the back of my armor.

Armor.

I let go of Kitten, but press my lips harder, trying to tell him without words that I don't want him to stop even though I'm taking my arms back. He's got no idea how to unbuckle foamed metal armor, it's a whole different mechanism than the cheap-ass ceramic plates.

His kisses have me shaking so hard I can barely work the buckles, but I wrench the shoulder straps undone, then the sides, and his arms loosen just enough that I can wrench the back plate away and fling it somewhere into the darkness.

It makes a glooping noise when it lands.

Right in the syrup? Two points, I guess.

Then I have to take my lips off his.

Kitten moans when I pull back.

The sound sets me on fire.

"Don't go anywhere," I whisper.

"Not a chance." It's not even a whisper—it's bare breath through his lips, like he can barely form words.

I pull back a little, weaseling the breast plate off, desperately yanking at the straps anchoring it into place.

World's most expensive body armor? Custom-tailored just for me?

Gloop.

I kiss him again, just a quick peck. I thought he was warm when I was wearing body armor, but now that I'm down to a T-shirt and bra he's on fire. The van isn't cold at all, I'm sweating and so is he and it's wonderful.

Kitten tries to pull me closer, and I can hardly think, but I push back again. "Just a minute," I say.

He trembles, but through my hand on his neck I feel him nod.

"Scoot back," I say. "Just a little."

I don't have time for this.

I don't want him to move away.

But he shifts a couple critical inches.

I quickly unstrap the armor that wraps around my groin and buttocks. It's supposed to come out the front, but that would mean getting Kitten to move back even more, and that just isn't happening, so I yank it out the back.

Ouch! Christ!

So *that's* why it's supposed to come out the front.

The last piece of armor follows the first two.

Three perfect shots in a row.

I drop back to the seat and yank Kitten close.

My hands are all over the warm beautiful smooth skin of his back, his chest, his face. His lips move on from mine, gently kissing and sucking at my neck. I've never felt anything that good, and my chin automatically rolls back to expose more of me for him.

Those big hands are tugging at the bottom of my shirt.

I wrap my legs around Kitten, holding him in to me. This time, I don't need to lock my ankles, he's not going anywhere.

I ripped his shirt apart to get it off his body earlier today. Can't he just do the same to mine?

Kitten freezes.

He's like a superheated statue in my arms.

"Should I stop?" he whispers.

"You stop," I growls, "and I will break your back where you are, Kitten."

A shudder ripples through him.

Oh, shit.

Death threats are not the proper response to absolutely everything.

"I'm sorry," I say out loud. I force a deep breath. My voice drops back to a whisper—I'm too embarrassed to say this part out loud, even in this all-devouring night. "I mean, you can stop if you want, you don't have to do anything. But I want you to take that shirt off of me. I really want you to. And... everything else."

He's still shuddering.

"If you want?" I finish, even more weakly.

I've ruined everything.

No, wait—he's not shuddering.

He's laughing.

Kitten is laughing at me.

"What's so funny?" I snarl, grabbing his shoulders.

"That," he chokes out, "is so. Perfectly. You."

His arms yank me close.

His mouth meets mine in the darkness.

20

I have never felt this peaceful.

The van's upturned flank is the most comfortable surface I've ever laid on.

Kitten might not know much about working as a freelancer.

But he has other skills.

I'm lying in his arms, he's lying in mine, we're this comfortable cozy tangle.

I'll never look at a banana the same way again.

Maybe I'll buy a banana farm.

Some indeterminate time later, though, I shift and open my eyes.

I can see the syrup pipe.

No, not with the infrared goggles. Who knows where those things are?

The pipe is painted orange.

Light shines down from above, past the pipe into the constantly renewed, constantly draining pool of syrup below.

The sight destroys my peace.

My bulletproof armor might be lying at the bottom of a pool of syrup.

But the important armor, the armor inside me?

That clangs right back into place.

This interlude... this break from being Liza Bradley... is over.

21

We get dressed in silence.

I don't look at Kitten. Now that there's light, I don't want to see his face when he looks at me.

I've heard all the jokes. Beer goggles. Pretty enough for two AM.

We'd been through two earthquakes in a twenty-four-hour period.

Been buried alive.

Life fighting death.

I get it. I really do.

I won't forget this. It's a night I'll lock away.

If anything like this ever happens again, I'll have a lot better idea what to do.

And some things won't be so surprising.

If someone asks me why I own a banana farm, I'll cut his throat.

My probing in the dark with the rifle barrel hit the back of a narrow little shaft. The oozing syrup pipe fills most of it.

If I grab hold of the steering wheel and hoist my head into the shaft, I can see an irregular square of blue sky.

There's one problem: the shaft is way too small for me to get through.

Kitten can probably weasel up through it just fine.

Maybe he can find something up there to shift that pipe.

Maybe he won't.

Maybe he can leave his ugliest, chunkiest fuck *ever* buried down here.

"I'll be back," Kitten says.

I'm not looking at his face. "I know you will."

The thing is, Kitten's a decent human being. He absolutely will come back. He will do absolutely everything he can to get me out of this hole.

We'll get out of this plant. Out of Guayaquil. Out of Ecuador.

And he never needs to see me again.

I still can't look at his face.

Kitten pauses, like he wants to say something.

But what is there to say?

But once his head's in the shaft, I can't help watching as he clambers up and into the light.

Away from me.

I have to sit and wait.

Alone.

That's usual, for me. Unless I'm fighting. Or training.

Somehow, the intimacy of throws and locks and grappling doesn't appeal as much.

I'll get over it.

I will.

The earpiece radio still doesn't work.

I should have thought to have Kitten take it up with him. Maybe it could reach the rest of the team once it didn't have all the rest of this on top.

No, he probably doesn't want to talk to them right now. Too many questions.

Even if they think nothing happened—of course they think nothing happened, how could anything happen with me—there's gonna be jokes. Someone's gonna rib Kitten about being stuck all night in the van with me. Ask him if he felt safe.

He's gonna blush like an apple again.

Those guys, they're not complete idiots. They'll figure it out in about two seconds flat.

It'll be a lot better for everyone if Kitten can get me out of here on his own.

Skip the obvious jokes.

Let him slink away.

In the meantime, I need to get myself together.

That mental sore's been lanced. All the pus drained out. It's okay to have a screaming fit now and then. Especially in the dark, or in private, or almost-private, when you're dancing with death.

Not to mention tangoing with life.

That is *not* helpful.

I sit, and shield myself.

In about forever, or maybe an hour, I hear Kitten shout. "Liza!"

Those mental shields?

Yeah, that one word slashes right through them.

I let myself quiver for the span of one breath, then grab hold of the steering wheel and shout back up. "Ki—*Harrison!*"

"This doesn't look good," he shouts, "but it's the best I can come up with."

"What's going on?"

"If I can get that syrup pipe out of the way, can you climb up?"

"Damn straight I can."

"I've got a long chain. And there's a truck nearby to hook it to. A couple girders that look like they're okay leverage. And that pipe, it's bent in a couple other places. I think—*think*—it'll shift if I pull it in the right spot."

"Then quit gabbing and get me the fuck out of this hole!"

"Hang on," he says. "The pipe, it's hooked up to one of those big tanks, I think. There's about a billion gallons of banana syrup in there. If this goes wrong, if I unkink the pipe, it might all—"

He can't say it.

Kitten's a fundamentally decent human being.

I wish I knew more of those.

I wish more of those *existed*.

He still can't say it.

I raise my voice. "If it breaks, I might drown in banana sewage. Got it. Do it."

"Or the rubble on top of you," he says. "It might shift. Finish falling."

"I understand," I say. "Do you have a better idea?"

"Go for help."

"Oh, yeah," I shout. "Excuse me, Mister Army Officer, my friend the freelance odd-job girl happens to be trapped in the food processing plant, you know, the one you closed off and put guards around? Think that's gonna work?"

Kitten doesn't say anything.

The anger and frustration runs out of me.

He doesn't deserve that.

Especially if this goes wrong.

Nobody deserves to get stuck with Liza Bradley.

"Kitten!" I shout. "I trust you. You see what's up there. You're the college boy. If you say it's the best shot, then do it."

"You sure?" he shouts.

My guts are quivering. "Absolutely," I say. "But hang on a minute."

"Yeah?" Kitten sounds… kind of hopeful?

"Can you remember something?"

"Sure."

"Anyone else around?"

A pause. "Uh… no?"

"Good." I try to speak very clearly. "Panama City, Panama. Bank of Central American Industry. Box three-six-nine-six-one-four. Repeat that back."

His voice is uncertain, but he repeats the number.

"The whole thing. City, bank, box number."

Now he sounds annoyed.

"Good," I call. "The box is in the name of Liza Fucking Bradley—yes, the 'fucking' is part of the name. Don't miss it, you've only got one chance to get this right."

I hear a distant, choked laugh.

"I'm serious. And you say the E-word as part of the name, they'll politely ask you to wait while they go get people to throw you into a deep dark cell. What I'm asking you to do is just as deadly as signing that contract."

"You can do it yourself, then," Kitten says.

"This is in case I can't," I say.

"I *will* get you out of there."

"Quit your meeping, Kitten, and pay attention! Or do I have to throw you around."

"No E-word." He sounds more sober now. "Panama City. Bank of Central American Industry. Box three-six-nine-six-one-four. Liza Fucking Bradley."

"Good." I can't believe I'm saying this. "The passcode is, and I quote. 'Come closer, my darling child. But not too close. For I, too, cannot be trusted.' Got it?"

"Passcode?" he shouts.

"It's French. Classic literature. Say it!" I snap.

He repeats it, omitting the *got it* at the end.

"Smart boy," I call. "Again. The whole thing."

I make him say it twice more before I'm satisfied.

A deep, shaking breath.

"If this goes wrong," I shout, "it's not your fault. Remember that. You go to the bank, ask for that box. Use my name and that code. There's documents in there. Bank records, passcodes. You take half of what's in there, send it to my folks."

"How do I find them?" he shouts.

"It's in the fucking box!" I bellow. "The other half—you take care of your mom. Your family. You get your fucking doctorate or something, go work in a lab."

I'm crying. Why am I crying? "And if you ever touch a goddamn weapon again, so help me, you are going to spend your days haunted by a banana ghost!"

I'd planned to leave my fortune to the Humane Society.

If this goes bad, it's all going to a single kitten.

Kitten doesn't say anything for a long breath. When he finally speaks, his voice shakes. "I'm getting you out of there."

"Go dry your eyes," I say. I need to take my own advice. "Man up, and get that pipe out of the ground so I can get the fuck out of this hole!"

It's silent so long that I think he's gone.

Then: "Thanks, Liza."

"Don't mention it. Really." My voice is strong again. I'm prouder than I should be. "But find a good martial arts school. Practice would do you some good."

Silence.

He really is gone.

The pinched end of the syrup pipe drips and oozes.

I wonder how quickly it'll start to gush.

Another forever later, though, I hear metal groan.

The pipe quivers.

Wobbles.

More syrup gushes from the end, like it's under pressure.

And slowly, so slowly, grinds its way up into the sky.

Spraying sticky, slippery banana all the way up.

22

The sky is beautiful, clear blue, scrubbed clean.

The sun casts warmth everywhere.

I am completely and utterly filthy.

The food processing plant?

Destroyed. A complete loss.

But my feet are on the ground, and the breeze is carrying the stink of that hole far, far away from me.

Kitten comes climbing over a broken chunk of concrete, ducking beneath a steel girder. He's moving quickly enough to be careless, and I want to yell at him to not break his neck.

But I still don't want to see his face when he looks at me.

So I turn to stare back towards the Pacific Ocean. It's out of sight, but I can smell it out there. Dead whales, rotting shrimp, and banana syrup.

"You all right?" Kitten says, maybe a yard behind me.

He's close enough I don't have to shout. Good.

The world doesn't need to hear this.

"I'm fine," I say. "Thanks for getting me out. The money's still yours, by the way."

"I don't care about the—"

"Oh yes you do!" I snarl. "You did all this to help your mom? You take the money and you do it. And you get the hell out of this business. You're too..." I wave a hand helplessly.

Clean. Decent. Something.

Something I'm not.

"Fine," he says.

"About down there," I say.

"I—"

"Shut up and listen!" I snap. "What happened—it was nice. It really was. But we were trapped. We thought we were going to die. We're human, it happens, and that's... that's okay. You meant it, I meant it, and that's fine, I know that."

I take a deep breath. It feels like I'm ripping my heart out of my chest.

"But you don't want to be with me. I get it. I really do. *I* don't want to be with me. That's fine. No harm, no foul."

I take a deep breath. "But you go bragging about bagging me, you even mention this ever again, and so help me—I will put you down like a rabid dog." A threat, a naked threat, should feel so much more comfortable, so familiar—but somehow even this feels like I'm stabbing myself right between the ribs with every word. "And I will make sure you see it coming. See it coming from a *long* way away."

Kitten doesn't say anything for a breath.

I stand there.

Then he asks politely, "Are you quite finished threatening me with slow death?"

I nod. "I think so. Yeah, I think so."

"Okay, then. You've had your piece. Now I'm going to say mine." His voice is tight.

Wow. Kitten sounds… mad. Actually angry?

"You have no idea what I feel like," he snaps. "You don't know what's in my head. You haven't even asked. The only thing you've done is threatened to break my back if I stopped kissing you, and then you won't even look at me." His words are sharper, more angry. "You know what I see when I look at you?"

I whirl. I'm looking at him now, and I've got a fist raised and cocked and ready to deck him.

Kitten looks just as mad as I do.

Maybe more so.

"I see the most loyal woman I've ever known," he spits. "She's capable, she's smart even if she won't give herself credit for it, she's got this great soft heart beneath a whole bunch of quills, and she's tired of lugging all that around on her own."

The world is spinning beneath me again.

But this earthquake is inside me.

Kitten steps closer. His blue eyes have this absolutely gorgeous rage in them.

But his voice gets quiet. Soft.

Tender.

"I see the kind of person I want to spend my life with."

I can't breathe.

"So," he says quietly. "It's up to you. If that's not what you want, that's okay. It's your choice. You say the word, I will take enough of your money to help my mom and say thank you and you will never hear from me again."

Kitten holds his arms apart.

No—he's opening his arms.

It's the worst earthquake yet.

I'm coming apart.

Blasting into a billion tiny pieces, yet staying in the exact same spot.

Kitten's whisper is barely audible above the Pacific wind.

"But if that sounds good to you… then all you have to do is say that word."

I'm shaking.

Forget the ground coming apart. Forget the mountain, gunfire, the thing with the bulldozer, even being buried alive.

I have never been so afraid in my life.

I can make the fear go away. I know how.

Climb over this rubble. Walk towards the ocean.

There's a whole world out there, waiting for me to blow it up.

My traitorous knees wobble.

I still can't breathe.

It's the hardest, bravest thing I've ever done.

I take one step towards Kitten.

I tip my head back.

Kitten's kiss is an earthquake on its own.

Liza Bradley first appeared in *Butterfly Stomp Waltz*.

About the Author
https://mwl.io

Never miss another new release!
Sign up for Michael Warren Lucas' mailing list at
http://mwl.io.

Novels:
Butterfly Stomp Waltz
Terrapin Sky Tango
Immortal Clay
Kipuka Blues
Hydrogen Sleets
git commit murder

Nonfiction (as Michael W Lucas):
Cash Flow for Creators – Relayd and Httpd Mastery – PAM Mastery
FreeBSD Mastery: Advanced ZFS
FreeBSD Mastery: Specialty Filesystems
FreeBSD Mastery: ZFS – Tarsnap Mastery
Networking for Systems Administrators
FreeBSD Mastery: Storage Essentials – Sudo Mastery
DNSSEC Mastery Absolute OpenBSD – SSH Mastery
Network Flow Analysis – Absolute FreeBSD
Cisco Routers for the Desperate – PGP & GPG
FreeBSD Mastery: Jails – Ed Mastery – SNMP Mastery

The Networknomicon

See your favorite bookstore for more!